➤➤➤➤➤

The Wonder in the Woods

The Wonder in the Woods

Patricia Cruzan

Patricia Cruzan

Cover Illustration by Kathaleen Brewer

Clear Creek Publishers
Fayetteville, Georgia

Printed by CreateSpace. The cover material and text are available only through permission of the publisher. The publisher is granted the use of the cover through a contract with the artist, Kathaleen Brewer.

The use of digital copies can only be approved for use through Clear Creek Publishers or Amazon.com.

First paperback edition 2013

Clear Creek Publishers

115 Clear Creek Court

Fayetteville, Georgia 30215

ISBN 978-0-9653543-7-0 (paperback)

Visit the author at www.patriciacruzan.com

➤➤➤➤➤➤➤

For my son

For people who love reading about pets,

sports, and friends

I am grateful to my husband, Chuck Cruzan, who helped

me put the book together, to Kathaleen Brewer for the cover

illustration,

to those who have read and offered book suggestions,

to Vicky Alvear Shecter, to SCBWI, to GWA, to SPAWN, and to

other writers.

Chapter

1

Boom! My last arrow missed the bull's-eye. The other ones in this end had missed the bull's-eye, too. When I first started archery, I tried to follow Coach Brown's tips. During my after-school practices, I've continued to use his tips. Becoming a professional will take lots of practice.

Ben and I made plans to practice today. I'd like to win the one thousand dollar prize in the competition coming up. Ben and I could split the prize money. We'd have to agree on that, though. The competition will be tough. Everyone has practiced for months.

At practice today, I looked over at Coach Brown after my first shot. I wanted him to notice how much I've improved. The coach had to watch the basketball players, so he didn't see my arrows. I kicked a few rocks around, hoping to get the coach's attention. The coach hadn't even looked over yet. For a little while, I asked Ben some questions. I wanted to delay our practice. My plan hadn't worked so far, since Ben took his position to start the game.

"Hold on. I need to talk to Coach Brown," I said.

"Hurry up! My mom wants me home early today," Ben said, tapping his foot. "Mom gave me chores to finish. On top of the chores, I have piles of homework."

I hurried over to where Coach Brown stood. When Ben had tapped his foot before, it showed he was impatient. I wanted encouragement: I'd flubbed my math test today. As I waited for the coach, I remembered grabbing the wrong book the night before the test. Having two books of the same color and size created a problem. I'd almost taken the wrong book another time, but I'd caught my error. This time, I hadn't noticed my mistake until it was too late. I had picked up my science book rather than my math book.

"Matthew Holliday," my teacher said in her stern voice.

I knew I was in trouble when I heard her say my name. Everyone usually called me Matt. As I stared at the big red *D* on my test paper, I knew I didn't want my parents to see the grade. Thinking about my parents' reactions made me sick. While I hurried back to my seat, my face felt warm, like a hot dog.

Now as I stood beside Coach Brown, I hoped to get his complete attention. I wanted to say the right words. Before I said anything, he asked me a question.

"What do you need, Matt?" he asked.

"Coach Brown, do you think I'm doing any better in archery?"

"Certainly. Why are you asking?"

"Could you look at my last shot on the target?"

"Did you make a bull's-eye?"

"No, but please look."

"If you'll wait a minute, I'll look. I need to dismiss the basketball players."

"Could you hurry? Ben needs to go home soon," I said. "I

want you to see my arrows before he shoots."

"Give me a minute," Coach Brown said.

When the coach dismissed the basketball players, I rushed with him toward the archery site. I wouldn't be able to stall Ben much longer. He was hurrying toward us.

I yelled, "Coach Brown is coming! Don't shoot yet. I want him to see my shots."

Everyone walked quietly while we rushed to the archery area. I watched the coach smile after he saw the target.

"Those shots are great ones! Several shots barely missed the bull's-eye."

"Thank you, Coach Brown," I said, as I grinned.

The coach stood on the archery range, waiting for Ben to shoot.

Ben stepped forward. He pulled the bow and released the arrow; his shots barely missed the bull's-eye, too.

"Whew, that was close," I said.

"The arrow could have landed an inch over," Ben said.

"It's close, but it's farther away than mine."

"No, they look like they are close to each other," Ben

said.

I didn't want to get into trouble, so I said nothing. Ben's friendship meant a great deal to me. I didn't want an argument.

"You both are doing great. Keep practicing. Practice helps," Coach Brown continued, while he walked away.

I took my position to release my arrows. At that moment, I heard a whimpering cry in the woods, so I stopped. Without saying anything, I darted into the woods. I wanted to know what had caused the noise.

"What are you doing? Finish your turn," Ben said.

I hurried back, whispering, "Hey, did you hear that noise?"

"No, Matt," said Ben. "What did it sound like? I didn't hear anything."

"It was a whimpering sound from the woods."

"Was it a two-footed or a four-footed sound?" Ben asked.

"I'm not sure," I replied, as we walked into the woods.

Coach Brown couldn't hear the rest of our conversation. He had basketballs to gather from the upper field. When he noticed us going into the woods, he yelled, "Stop! Why are you entering the woods? That area's off limits."

"We heard something; we wanted to check it out." I said.

"Wait for me. You shouldn't go into the woods without an adult. I'll go in first," Coach Brown said.

As the coach tried to catch up with Ben and me, an eerie silence fell over the wooded area. The sky grew dark, and the sun hid behind the clouds. I saw tree shadows shifting with the whoosh of the wind. Without any warning, another series of small cries rang out.

"Get back!" Coach Brown shouted.

Before the coach uttered another word, a dog appeared. I reached down to stroke it, without realizing the dog might be protecting its puppies.

"If the dog is nursing its young, it might bite. Be careful about touching the mother dog and her puppies. Animals protect their babies, like humans protect their young ones," Coach Brown said.

Ben had kneeled to pet the mother dog, too, but he stopped after the coach's warning. Ben moved farther back.

"I think the dog's hungry. I wonder how long it's been

out here," Ben said.

"Let's get some dog food," I suggested.

"I'll keep an eye on the dog. You boys go find food and water for it," Coach Brown said. "Get back as quickly as possible, but be careful."

I nodded to the coach. "Ben can help me get dog food at Hannah's; her house is just across the street."

"We're not going to a girl's house to get dog food!" Ben protested.

"What's wrong with that?" I asked.

"I don't want to go to a girl's house. Matt, girls are always talking; besides, Hannah might be practicing the piano. Let's go to Jake's house," Ben said.

"That's fine. Hannah loves dogs, though. She'd help us out."

"I don't care where you go. Just get some food for the dog. I need to get home," Coach Brown said. "My wife will have dinner shortly."

"Let's go to Jake's," Ben said.

We raced to Jake's house. Right before I rang the

doorbell, Jake flung the door open. Luckily I stepped back in time, before he trampled me. When he stopped, he greeted me like he normally did.

"What's up, Matt?" Jake asked.

"We found a dog behind the school. Could you get water and food for it?" I asked.

"I'll get my mom to help. I'm late for my trumpet lesson," Jake said.

"We could go some place else," I replied.

"You don't need to do that. Mom will help, because Dad is waiting for me. I'll get her."

After Jake's mom, Mrs. Graham, appeared at the door, I explained why I needed dog food. Once she let us in, Ben and I followed her to the garage to get the food. While we gathered the dog food, we discussed ways of finding the dog's owner.

"We can make signs to put on telephone poles," I said.

"What about putting an ad in the newspaper?" Mrs. Graham asked.

"That costs money. I have five dollars. How much do you have, Ben?"

"I have about three dollars. Maybe the kids in our class could chip in," Ben suggested.

"We need to find the owner. The dog looks like it's been washed and brushed lately."

"The dog does look clean. Its coat doesn't look too matted," Ben said.

I really wanted the dog, but I knew we had to look for its owner. I didn't know what my parents might think about getting a dog.

As Ben and I started to leave, I thanked Mrs. Graham for her help. We rushed back to school to get the dog fed.

Before Ben and I thought of other ways to find the dog's owner, we were on the school grounds. We hurried to find the coach, dog, and puppies, because it was getting really dark. The minute the coach set the food in front of the dog, it gobbled the food up. Afterwards, the dog lapped every drop of water set out for it.

I didn't want to leave the dog. Coach Brown observed how thirsty the dog was, so he found more water to pour into the dog's dish. He sent Ben and me home. All the way home, I tried to devise a plan to get the dog. I knew tonight wouldn't be a good time to mention the dog at home, since I had problems with my test paper. *Of course, the dog might take my parents' minds off the test grade.* That was a possibility. As Ben and I walked together, I said very little.

➤

Chapter

2

Once Ben arrived at his house, I ran home. Mom wanted me to

be there by six o'clock. I had five minutes to get home. To be

able to participate in fun activities, I had to mind Mom. I'd found

that being grounded was no fun.

After I arrived at home, I scrubbed my hands.

Immediately, I set the table for dinner. I knew it was almost time

to eat, because Mom had two serving bowls of food on the table.

She had chicken that she'd just placed on a platter. I figured if I

helped her now, I'd have more time to finish chores and to read

books later. At dinner, I wasn't that hungry.

"You aren't eating like you usually do," Mom said. "Are you sick?"

"No," I said. "I have lots to do."

I pushed my chair away from the table. I stood up and walked away. I didn't get far, because Mom stopped me.

"If you don't feel like eating, you need to go to *bed*."

I didn't like to hear the word bed, so I sat down to eat. My normal bedtime was three hours from now; I didn't want to be stuck in bed. I hadn't stopped thinking about the dog and the puppies, since Jake, Coach Brown, and I had found the dogs. I knew the dogs needed help, because their owner was missing. At my house, my parents hadn't mentioned getting a dog; I didn't think they wanted one. With Ben and Jake's help, the dog didn't have to be hungry, though. Each of us could feed the dog twice a week, and I could feed it on the extra day, too. I'd have to get Mom and Dad to agree to my plan. I had another concern: the puppies. They would need a veterinarian's attention. I knew Hannah's puppies had to be checked after birth. I didn't know how to get the money to care for them, though.

Before working on my homework, I telephoned Ben.

While I waited for him to answer the phone, I searched the phone book for a veterinarian's number. I knew a veterinarian wasn't cheap; I'd overheard Hannah's mother tell my mother how expensive a veterinarian was. My allowance was at an all-time low. I waited patiently for Ben to answer his phone.

"Hello, Matt," Ben said.

"How'd you know it was me?"

"Mom checks caller ID when the phone rings. I can't talk long, because my mom wants me to study for my test."

"Oh, I forgot about another test. I was calling about the dog. Each of us could feed the dog two days this week, while we look for the owner. I can feed it the extra day," I said. "I'm going to look for a veterinarian for the puppies."

"I don't think my mom will mind. Did your mom agree for you to do that?" Ben asked.

"I haven't asked yet, but I don't think there will be a problem."

"Tomorrow, I'll let you know if I can help. I have to get off the phone. Mom is calling me," Ben said.

I knew my mom might call me soon. Each night she

liked to look over my homework, so I hurried to call Jake. I felt relieved when he answered on the second ring. Before I said why I'd called, Jake mentioned the dog. He promised that he'd help me feed it. When we finished talking, I told him that I needed to call a veterinarian for the puppies.

The first veterinarian call didn't go well. For six weeks of puppy care, I would owe more than my allowance for a year.

I punched in the numbers for Dr. Thompson, another veterinarian. He consented to help with the puppies, if my friends and I cared for the mother dog. He agreed to give the grown dog a checkup. If it had no health problems, my friends and I would feed and water the dog every day. If its owner didn't claim the grown dog, then the dog needed to be adopted. I thought we had a solution, but we hadn't discussed the puppies' shots yet. I was almost afraid to mention them, since I knew they weren't cheap. Before I hung up, Dr. Thompson and I had worked out a plan.

The puppies would receive their first shots free. They would stay at the veterinarian's for a few days. The adopted parents would have to pay for the next round of shots. I had no money to pay for them.

Just when I thought the plan would work, I faced another hurdle. There wasn't much time to find people to adopt them. At least I'd made progress with Dr. Thompson.

When I hung up the phone, I began making a list of people who might want a puppy. My plans came to a screeching halt before I could carry them out.

"Matt, are you getting your homework?" Mom questioned.

"I'll do it," I promised.

"I thought you got your books out twenty minutes ago. Get busy. I'll check your homework in an hour. I want a good grade on your test tomorrow."

Mom wanted me to do well on everything. The other subjects were easy, but I actually had to study math. I had other things to do, too. I lifted my books from my backpack, and then I studied the sample math problem. It didn't take long to work through a row of problems. When I felt I needed a break, I slipped downstairs for a snack. I must have made too much noise, because Mom called me.

"Matt, are you ready for me to check your homework?"

"Not yet," I said. "But, I've been working on math."

"Why aren't you ready?" Mom asked.

"I was studying. I'm taking a snack break."

"You can get a snack, but don't take too long. You need to go to bed early tonight."

I hadn't mentioned the dog and puppies to Mom yet. While I had her attention, I explained what had happened at school. Once I asked for permission to help feed the dog, Mom agreed. I told her what I'd worked out with Dr. Thompson. I also shared my previous test paper with her. I let Mom know how I'd picked up the wrong book to study from. She didn't respond like she usually did. I figured Mom's solemn look showed her disappointment, but she only made a few comments.

"I know the dogs need help, but your school grades need to improve. You may need to stop some of your extra activities. I understand how you took the wrong book home, so I won't ground you this time. If it happens again, you will be grounded."

"I'll do better, Mom. Thanks for giving me another chance, since I made a mistake."

With three peanut butter crackers, I returned to my desk. I

gobbled the first one. As I reached for the second one, I stopped when the phone rang. I ran to answer it, but Mom beat me to it.

I never heard Mom say who'd called, so I went to my room. I finished eating the last peanut butter cracker, and I returned to my homework.

In thirty minutes, Mom knocked on my bedroom door. Once my homework was checked, Mom mentioned Ben's phone call. She told me how Ben had agreed to help feed the golden retriever.

When I discovered Ben and Mom had worked out a feeding schedule, I breathed a sigh of relief. Then, I returned to look over my list of people who might want a puppy.

Of course, the puppy problem would be solved, if the dog's owner would claim it. If the owner didn't show up, the coach would place an ad in the newspaper. Right now, I was happy to be getting help with the dog and puppies from my friends.

➤

Chapter

3

The next morning I overslept, so Mom came into my room to wake me. She shook me to get me up. By the time I reached Ben's house, he'd gone. I knew I had to hurry to make school on time. I ran fast to get there.

I looked forward to today, because the teacher had a guest coming. During math time, the speaker planned to show us what was happening in technology. If the program lasted a long time, I knew there wouldn't be time for the math test. The speaker's remarks didn't last as long as I'd hoped, though. When the speaker left, the teacher passed out the test. I worked hard, checking over each problem. I wanted to make an *A*. My average needed bringing up before report cards went out. By the end of the test, I knew I'd done my best.

When all test papers were handed in, we went outside. During physical education, I scored two goals in soccer. A dog's bark in the distance sent me running toward the woods. I didn't get far, because my teacher, Ms. Winthrop, stopped me.

"You know we don't go into the woods," she said. "What are you doing?"

At that moment, I realized I hadn't told her anything about the dog in the woods. I shared several details about the dog with her. Ms. Winthrop told me that our class might be able to help the dog, but she wanted us to check with the principal. Once I had a pass for the principal, Mr. Henry, I headed to his office. When I arrived there, he had stepped out. I knew I'd have to come back later, because he was in a meeting.

The rest of the day, I had trouble doing my schoolwork. I was daydreaming: my thoughts were on the dog and its puppies.

After the final school bell rang for the day, Ben, Jake, and I headed to the woods. We wanted to check on the dogs. Before we entered the woods, we made sure no one saw us. I'd been unable to get the principal's permission to go to the woods. I hadn't had enough time to stop by his office again. As soon as we stepped into the woods, someone yelled at us.

"Hey, what are you kids doing?" the custodian asked.

When I told the custodian, Mr. Bentley, about the talk with Ms. Winthrop, he agreed to let us see the dogs. I didn't tell him the part about getting it approved through the principal. Ben, Jake, and I stayed in the woods for ten minutes, checking on the dogs. When we were sure no one was watching us, I picked up one puppy to take home. I planned to talk Mom into letting me have the puppy. The veterinarian planned to pick up the other puppies at six o'clock.

As soon as Mom saw the puppy, she made me take it back to the woods. I placed the puppy with its mother. Not being able to keep the puppy brought tears to my eyes. I cried silently all the way home.

The next day, Mom told me about the pet ad she'd seen in the newspaper. Mom handed me the ad to see after I asked for it. I looked over the ad, and I decided Coach Brown put it in the paper. Seeing the ad made me want to talk my parents into getting a dog. I had to find people to adopt the puppies. If the people who'd owned the mother dog didn't show up, I'd have to find it a home as well. My friends and I would be spending lots of time taking care of the mother dog for a while. The veterinarian had taken the puppies to care for until they were adopted.

At the end of the week, I went to see Coach Brown. He told me that no one had claimed the grown dog. It was hard to imagine anyone not wanting it; the dog was friendly and beautiful.

After two weeks passed, the coach placed another ad in the newspaper. This ad had bold letters at the top to attract a person's attention. The price for each puppy was low. I figured the veterinarian's phone wouldn't stop ringing. That didn't happen.

No one had purchased any puppy by Friday. I knew that Dr. Thompson and Coach Brown didn't plan on making money from the sales. *Why didn't people purchase the puppies?*

I decided to try something new to find homes for the

dogs. I rang the neighbors' doorbells for blocks. By letting everyone know about the dogs, I hoped to find the dog's owner. People might be willing to adopt one of its puppies, too. I had little time left to get them placed. After my door-to-door visits, I still had no owners for the dogs.

➤

Chapter

4

At school, my friends and I talked before class. Friends shared a funny story that happened before school. I found out how the teacher's helper, Lynn, knew the details. After Lynn stepped from the girls' restroom, I questioned her.

"What happened this morning in our classroom?" I asked.

"I heard strange noises. When I finished a job for Ms. Winthrop, I looked around the classroom. I searched the back corner, and I found a golden retriever on Cindy's coat. I didn't know what to do."

"What happened then?"

"I tried pulling the coat from under the dog's belly," Lynn said. "The dog didn't budge. I pulled the coat again, but I stopped when the coat started to rip."

"Did the dog leave?"

"No. When I moved to the middle of the room, Ms. Winthrop's eyes met mine. I didn't know whether she had heard the noise or not."

"Did you get into trouble?" I asked.

"No. The teacher didn't see the dog, because she was sitting down grading papers. I said nothing about the dog being there, because I didn't want the retriever to be taken out. The teacher questioned me after hearing a noise."

"What did she ask?"

"She asked, 'What were you reaching for?' "

"What did you say?" I asked.

"Cindy's coat was on the floor. I was trying to pick it up."

"What happened then?"

"When Ms. Winthrop returned to her paper grading, I tried getting the dog out by giving it a treat. A whimper from the dog caused Ms. Winthrop to look up again. Before I said anything, the dog walked toward her," Lynn said.

"Did Ms. Winthrop put the dog out?"

"The teacher pushed the red buzzer in the room. She said, 'Get Mr. Bentley.' By the time he arrived, the dog had disappeared. I told no one about it following me to the restroom, because I didn't want the dog found."

"Did Mr. Bentley find the dog?"

"I don't think so," Lynn said.

"I hope not. My friends and I are taking care of the grown dog in the woods," I said.

"Why are you doing that? Doesn't the dog have a home?" Lynn asked.

"No one has claimed it. The dog's gentle. Would you like to adopt it or a puppy?" I asked.

"A puppy sounds like fun, but I'll have to check with my mom," Lynn said.

"Will you…?" I began.

"Quit talking," Ms. Winthrop interrupted. "Go into the classroom and get your materials ready."

I obeyed. The teacher started the reading groups. Then, she opened the classroom door. While I sat in the reading group, a shadow moved across the floor. From a distance, the shadow looked like a dog. When it wandered close to me, I snickered. The snickering noise caused my friends to look up. Before long, the whole class was laughing.

"Read the rest of the story silently," Ms. Winthrop said in her edgy voice.

In a few minutes, the teacher pushed the buzzer to alert Mr. Bentley of the dog's return. Mr. Bentley tried to catch the dog once he arrived. Every time Mr. Bentley moved close to it, the dog plopped down. There was no way to get it to move. The class laughed. Mr. Bentley made other attempts to remove the dog, but he had no success. He finally decided to get someone else to help him.

"Ms. Winthrop, we need the dogcatcher," Mr. Bentley said.

"Wait a few minutes. Maybe the dog will leave soon. I'll buzz you again, if it doesn't leave," the teacher said.

My friends and I smiled while the dog moved among us. I

watched it act like it belonged there. In a few minutes, the dog rested its head on its paws. My teacher didn't buzz the office again. I thought she'd forgotten about the dog. She lined us up, and she left the dog still in the classroom.

Once my class left our hall, I slipped back to the classroom. I planned to lead the dog from the room. When I first stepped back into the room, I didn't see the dog. I saw its tail flop, though.

I petted the dog. I got it to follow me by throwing my snack out the back door. The dog leaped for the snack, so I jumped back into the building. I quickly closed the door. I didn't want the dog to jump inside.

➤

Chapter

5

I hurried to catch up with my class, but I didn't make it before a stranger was on my hall. Immediately, an alarm sounded, because the man hadn't signed in at the office. Every student scurried to a safety spot. My school was on lockdown.

Before long, I heard an announcement over the speaker system. The stranger turned out to be the dogcatcher. Everyone returned to what they had been doing prior to the alarm. I wanted to know if the dogcatcher had caught the dog. I smiled after I heard the news: the dog was still on the loose.

I wanted the dog to be safe in the woods. At least, I'd

been able to help it before the dogcatcher arrived.

During the afternoon, we finished class assignments and had story time. My class had a science discussion on mammals before physical education. By participating in the discussion, I discovered how dogs differed from other animals. Ms. Winthrop had Ben and me gather the baseball equipment for my class.

Once everyone was outside, my teacher selected team captains. The captains chose their team players. Ben and I ended up on the same team. Not having Jake on my team made me feel less confident, since his team usually won. Ben and Mark hit a home run on my team after twenty minutes. I thought my team might win. The score was four to two, in our favor.

I took my position at home plate. On the first pitch, I hit a foul ball. I slugged the ball to center field on the second pitch. I knew I had a home run. Then the unexpected happened: the golden retriever leaped in the air. Before anyone stopped the dog, it grabbed the ball. The retriever ran away with it. Without the baseball, the game stopped.

I watched the dog run to Cindy. When Cindy tried to grasp the ball, the golden retriever yanked its head away. The dog's actions reminded me of playing a *keep-away* game. I ran to help Cindy get the ball, so the dog didn't disappear with it. Each time I reached for the ball, the dog jerked its head away. I was determined to get the ball.

My classmates, standing behind me, laughed at the dog's antics. I chased the dog for a while, and I managed to get the ball. The sound of Ms. Winthrop's shrill whistle blowing stopped me. The whistle sound signaled the end of the class period. Once I stood in line, my face felt on fire. I stomped my foot in anger, because the dog had kept me from scoring. Jake's comment made me angry, too.

"That dog knows how to help your team. Did you train it to do that?" Jake asked.

"How do you figure that? You've been with the dog as much as I have," I said. "The dog didn't help us. It kept us from making another home run. The dog stole the ball from my team."

"I was kidding," Jake said.

"I'm glad the dogcatcher didn't catch the dog, but I don't like to have it in the baseball game."

"We have enough trouble getting the ball without the dog

grabbing it. I'd like to have it as a pet. I wouldn't want it to interfere with our game," Jake said.

I sealed my lips when Ms. Winthrop glared in my direction. I didn't want to run a few laps after school for talking. I'd had to run them before. Even though the dog kept me from making a home run, I had a soft spot in my heart for the retriever. I couldn't be mad at the dog for long. Before I followed my class inside, I saw the dog slinking into the woods. I noticed its tail tucked between its legs. The dog seemed to sense it had done something wrong.

I knew Jake liked the dog, because he'd spent lots of time petting it. Since I couldn't keep the dog, I hoped Jake could. Of course, I planned to ask my parents again about its adoption.

➤

Chapter

6

My mom knew I had archery practice after school, so I didn't call her. I arrived at the field and checked in with the coach. As I took my archery position, I listened for sounds coming from the woods. I heard nothing, so I started practicing.

Before shooting my arrows, I moved slowly, trying to use the coach's tips. As I placed the arrow into the bow, I aimed right at the bull's-eye. My arrow landed within an inch of it.

By the time I'd finished shooting my first end, Jake dashed from the back of the school building. I listened as he told why he was delayed. He'd had to give his corrected math paper to the teacher.

Jake set his school bag down close by, stepping up to shoot arrows. His arrows landed a short distance from the bull's-eye.

On my second end, I felt Jake's eyes on me. He stood five feet away, but said nothing. Finally, on my last shot of the second end, I hit the bull's-eye.

"I did it!" I screamed in my excitement.

"You don't have to brag. I see it," Jake said.

"I've practiced so much. Can't you be happy for me?" I asked.

"Hitting the bull's-eye is a reward. I don't have to congratulate you every time, do I?"

"No, but it's nice for you to cheer me on. I'm sure you can hit the bull's-eye, too. Try it."

Jake moved over to shoot for his second end. He frowned after he missed the bull's-eye on each shot.

"Your arrow's close to the target," I said, trying to encourage him.

"I don't know. That arrow is several inches away."

"Your shots are getting better."

Jake and I practiced for an hour. Near the end of the practice, he hit the bull's-eye. Now it was his turn to scream, but he didn't scream as loudly. When the practice ended, Jake and I started home. We discussed the school festival to be held in two days.

Before Jake and I left each other, we set up a time for our next practice. I ran to get home; I wanted to watch television later. When I heard a branch pop behind me, my heart raced. I knew the branch didn't pop on its own, so I hurried down the path. There had been no recent storm, weakening tree branches. When I sped up, something behind me sped up. My heart pounded, making it hard to tell what was going on. Every now and then I'd hear a pop. I knew something was still there. I didn't slow down until I arrived on my front porch. At my front door, I yelled loudly. Every door within half a block, including my mom's, flew open.

"What's wrong?" Mom asked.

"Let me in!" I cried out.

"I see the golden retriever came with you. Why is it

here?"

I turned around to see the familiar dog wagging its tail. Once I realized the dog had followed me, my heartbeat slowed down. Rather than a person stalking me, there stood my favorite dog, looking for attention. I must have missed the dog at first, because Jake and I were talking.

"Doesn't the dog have a home yet?" Mom questioned.

"No, but I'd like to have the dog."

"I'm sure you would, but its owner might be looking for the retriever. Whose turn is it to feed the dog tonight?"

"It's my turn," I said.

"Your father will help take the dog to the wooded area. I'm surprised its family hasn't claimed it. She's pretty and good-natured. The ad has appeared in the newspaper for several days."

"Mom, couldn't we keep the dog?" I pleaded.

"I don't want to take another person's dog."

"What if no one claims it?"

"We'll deal with that later. Right now, get it inside and close the door. Keep it by the door while I get Dad. He'll get a leash for the dog. Then, you can help Dad take it to the woods."

When Dad joined us, we headed to the woods with the dog. The dog cried for attention when we started to leave it. I kneeled down to pet the dog. Even though it didn't belong to me, I loved the dog. My eyes became misty, but I didn't want Dad to see them.

I was grateful Dad let me pet the dog before we left. After spending a few minutes with it, Dad and I hurried to the car. We wanted to get home before dark. While I rode home with Dad, he asked questions about archery practice. The questions took my mind off the dog for a few seconds, but I didn't want to discuss archery.

"It sounds like you're making progress in archery. Keep at it," Dad said.

"I will," I replied.

At that moment, I just wanted to rescue the dog. I knew some dogs ended up being put down. I didn't know if Dad knew what happened to many dogs or not, but I wanted to save this one's life.

Chapter

7

At school, I finished my morning work early. My teacher let me go to the library. I chose a nonfiction book on dogs to read. While I read the book, I fell more in love with the golden retriever. I knew Mom and Dad didn't seem to want the mother dog now. Perhaps they'd change their minds. I liked the puppies, too, but the older dog was my favorite.

Going to the library was fun, so I followed my teacher's instructions to stay only thirty minutes. I looked forward to the math activity in class today. The written math work wasn't as interesting to me as some things, but the group work sounded like fun.

During math, each group of four had to make up math problems to solve and share. After thirty minutes, each person shared one problem with the group. My group had a tie when we voted. Two students voted for Cindy's problem and two classmates voted for mine. The group decided to look at the problems again; they voted a second time. I received three votes this time, so I won the prize. I chose a book from the teacher's gift pile: a book on pet care.

Before walking home from school, my friends and I searched for the large retriever. I wanted to pet it. I decided it was safe to go to the dog, because Mr. Bentley was sweeping on another hall. From the times I'd helped Ms. Winthrop after school, I knew it took Mr. Bentley thirty minutes on each hall. My friends and I figured I'd have enough time to pet the dog.

When Ben, Jake, and I entered the woods, I didn't find the dog in its usual spot. Once I found it, I didn't stay long. My parents wanted me home at quarter past three. I wanted to check on the dog, but I hoped to avoid Mr. Bentley's eyes. My friends and I didn't want a trip to the principal's office. In two hours, I planned to meet Coach Brown for a baseball game. I'd heard Jake mention asking the girls to play, but I didn't want them to play with us. Most of the girls in our class didn't bat like the guys did; they liked to chat, too. I didn't mind playing with them when Lynn told jokes. Her jokes made me laugh until my belly hurt. I didn't hear her say that she'd play with us today.

As I arrived home, I started on my chores. I wanted to walk with my friends to the baseball field later. We had agreed to meet at Jake's. Once my friends arrived at his house, we walked and talked together to the baseball game.

At school, I found out that the girls were playing with us. When it was my turn to bat, I made two strikes. I hit a ball to center field on my third try. Before I rounded the first base, the golden retriever grabbed the ball. I watched the dog with disgust, because the other team laughed and laughed.

"That would have been a home run, but the dog grabbed it. My hit should count as a home run," I said.

"Well, what makes you think it would be a home run? Someone may have tagged you. That would have been an out," Lynn said.

"It's not fair!" I yelled.

"What's not fair?" Lynn asked.

"The dog didn't grab your batted ball, making *you* forfeit a home run," I said.

"That's true. The dog's picked you as its owner. Can't you tell?" Lynn asked.

"That's right," Hannah chimed in.

"The dog isn't mine." I said angrily.

"It's your dog," Hannah said.

"No, it isn't. My parents won't let me have a dog right now."

Everyone quieted down. The silence was broken when the dog came close to everyone. My friends and I petted the dog. I watched the golden retriever wander off again. With the dark clouds rolling in, I hurried to leave. Mom didn't like me out after dark. In my haste to leave, I failed to pick up my coat; I left it on the playground. As I ran away, I used my shirt to wipe the sweat from my brow. I didn't wait for my friends. For the time being, I didn't want to be around anyone. I didn't want to be kidded about the grown dog that I wanted.

➤

Chapter

8

During the evening meal, I kept quiet. I wanted to hurry to feed

the golden retriever. The dog had sniffed everything in sight

earlier. As Dad set his napkin on the table, I stood up to get his

attention.

"Dad, are you ready to go feed the dog?" I asked.

"Get the food ready. By the time you finish gathering

everything, I will be."

I poured the dog food in a dish and put water in a jug. To

keep the dog food from spilling out, I covered the dog dish with

one of Mom's plastic tops. Before Dad joined me outside, I saw something in the distance on the grass. The colors looked familiar, so I set the dog's containers down. I stepped forward, looking at the coat on the grass; I recognized it as mine. I knew I hadn't left it where it was. Several seconds passed, and then I recalled leaving the coat on the school playground. I'd been too hot playing, so I'd taken it off. As I looked at my coat, a familiar face greeted me with golden hair and sparkling eyes. I stroked the dog's fur. When I spoke to the dog, Dad cut in.

"I see the dog is at our house again. Did it follow you home?"

"I didn't see the dog follow me. It seems to know the way here."

"Why is your coat on the grass? It doesn't belong there. Mom won't like having to wash it because of your carelessness."

"I'm not sure how the coat ended up in our yard. During the school game, I took it off. I started sweating. I don't think I had it with me when I left school."

"Don't lose your coat. You don't want to use your allowance money to replace it, do you?"

"I'll try to be more careful. I think I left it on the school playground. When I left school this afternoon, the sky was gray. The coat was several yards from me. I didn't see it on the ground, so I must have forgotten about it. I'm not sure how it landed in our yard."

"I think I know how," Dad said.

"How?"

"Well, judging from the dirt on it, I'd say the dog dragged it here. I hope there aren't any holes on it. Didn't your mother buy that coat a month ago?"

"I think it's been longer. I'm sorry, Dad."

"Take better care of your coat. You might not get it back next time," said Dad. "That dog is starting to look too comfortable here."

"May we keep it, Dad?"

"I don't think so, but your mom and I will discuss it. We haven't planned on getting a dog now. The family vacation is coming soon. The golden retriever is too big to go with us. Boarding her would cost us extra money."

"Please, Dad, let's keep the grown dog."

"The dog sees you as its master, but we're not keeping it.

The dog belongs to someone. The owner just hasn't shown up yet. The dog might have to become a new family's dog."

Dad and I left to take the dog to the woods. As I followed Dad, my eyes glazed over with tears. It was painful to share the dogcatcher incident with Dad, but I did. Even though my father listened, he didn't change his opinion about keeping the dog. I dreaded having to find it a new home.

I telephoned several people that night, trying to find puppy homes. The veterinarian had agreed to keep the puppies for only a few days. One puppy might have a home. That meant four dogs would need a home: one dog was the mother dog. The veterinarian's deadline for finding puppy homes was close. I had to find a way to get the other dogs a home.

➤

Chapter

9

The sun's rays peeking through my curtains made me pull the covers over my head. I wanted to sleep, but was unable to. Mom's voice called from a distance, listing the chores I needed to do. I tried to tune her out, but I heard her next announcement clearly.

"The pancakes are ready," Mom said.

I hurried to eat my favorite breakfast. When Dad asked about homes for the puppies, I hated to tell him.

"I've called and visited people, but only one puppy might have a home," I said.

While the family continued to eat, Dad didn't say much. I started to leave the table, and then Dad volunteered to help me look for puppy homes. I thanked him and left. When I stepped into my room, the doorbell sounded.

"See who is at the door," Dad called out.

I ran to open the front door. To my surprise, some classmates greeted me.

"Hello, Matt," Jake and Hannah said.

My jaw dropped when I saw Hannah with Jake. I knew Jake didn't hang out with girls. I invited them inside after I got over the shock of seeing them together. Jake stepped in, but Hannah lingered by the door.

"I'll wait here a few minutes," Hannah said. "I came to check on adopting a puppy. My mother told me I could have one. Where are the puppies?"

"Dr. Thompson, one of the town veterinarians, has the puppies. I can get his number for you. If you want me to, I can call him."

"While you call the veterinarian, I'll step in. I can't stay, because my mom wants me to shop with her."

I dashed to my room, grabbing the phone and the veterinarian's number. When I returned, I interrupted Jake and Hannah's conversation about the golden retriever. It was unusual to see them talking, because during the school year Jake didn't talk to girls. I decided they had one thing in common: they liked dogs.

Hannah grinned when I gave her the information she needed, and she thanked me. Even though I didn't usually talk to girls, my mood had improved. Hannah had agreed to take one of the puppies. Of course, playing ball with girls was something totally different than adopting puppies. They usually didn't hit balls as far as my friends did. I walked Hannah to the door, trying to be polite. I waved good-bye as she walked away.

Jake and I talked a few minutes, but he had to leave soon. His mother had something she wanted him to do at home.

I whistled as I walked back to my bedroom. I still had to find homes for the other puppies, so I reached for the phone book. Before I punched in another number, the phone rang. At first I couldn't figure out who was on the other end. I heard a scratchy sounding voice.

"Matt," Cindy said, stretching out the vowel in my name.

"What do you want?" I asked.

I felt my face turn hot like a firecracker. The way she said my name irritated me. I didn't want my friends to know Cindy had called me, either. There were enough problems in my life without girls. I was thankful Jake wasn't at my house anymore. I had other work to do, so I tried to get her off the phone. Before I started to hang up, I heard the word puppies.

"Hannah told me about the puppies at Dr. Thompson's," Cindy said.

"So, would you like one, too?" I asked.

"Maybe. Mom told me we might get one. Will you give me the number of the veterinarian who has the dogs?"

"Are you really going to get one?"

"Mom is thinking about getting me a puppy," Cindy said.

"Hold on. I'll get the veterinarian's number."

When I looked around my room, I discovered that I'd misplaced Dr. Thompson's number. I didn't want Cindy to change her mind, so I realized I'd have to call her back quickly.

"Cindy, I've misplaced the veterinarian's number. Could

I call you when I find it? I'll need your number."

"My number is 555-555-2310. I'll let you go, so you can find the number."

Before I found Dr. Thompson's number, I searched my desktop, pants pockets, and bed. I didn't see the number, so I walked back toward the front door. I'd given the information to Hannah earlier. The phone number slip wasn't on the living room table; it had fallen on the floor. Once I found it, I returned to my room to call Cindy. When a voice answered Cindy's phone, I could tell it wasn't Cindy's voice.

"Hello," a lady's voice answered.

"I'm . . . I'm . . . calling for Cindy," I said nervously.

"She's not here. I can write your number down for her to call you later. I'm her mother, Mrs. Little."

I told Mrs. Little the veterinarian's name and mine, and I gave her our phone numbers and addresses. While she wrote the information down, I waited on the line. Talking to a girl was bad enough, but talking to her mother was worse. After I hung up, questions popped in my mind. *Would Cindy call back? Would Dad kid me about her? Would Cindy talk to me at school? That would be terrible.* After all, boys my age thought girls were like aliens.

Finding a football magazine, on my bed, helped me forget about the conversation with Cindy's mom. I thumbed through the magazine, looking for the article about my hero. I became so engrossed in it that football was the only thing on my mind.

➤

Chapter

10

I read until Mom announced company. Having company this time of night was unusual; in an hour, it would be my bedtime. The company provided a perfect excuse to stay up late, so I tiptoed to the family room. When I entered the room, a classmate sat on the sofa talking to Mom. Even though I didn't know Cindy's mom, I knew the lady sitting beside Cindy must be related to her; the two looked just alike.

At first, I didn't say anything. I listened while Mom explained the reason for Mrs. Little and Cindy's visit. Carrying on a conversation with a girl was difficult, but having two moms there made it more difficult. I waited twenty seconds, and then I gathered the courage to speak.

"How can I help you?" I asked.

"Before we purchase a dog from Dr. Thompson, I'd like to ask you some questions," Mrs. Little said, smiling.

I sat on the edge of the sofa as I answered the questions. To be sure Mrs. Little understood everything, I shared details and pictures of the puppies. I relaxed after Mrs. Little decided on a female puppy. Cindy and Mrs. Little left after I answered all their questions.

"You didn't mention having a girlfriend. I didn't think you liked girls," Dad said, solemnly.

"They are all right. I don't have a girlfriend."

"Cindy smiled and talked to you a lot," Dad kidded.

"She dropped by to discuss getting one of the puppies."

"Why didn't she call rather than come by?"

"I called her with the information needed, but she wasn't home. Mrs. Little wrote the information down."

"I think Cindy likes you, since she came over," Dad said. "She could have telephoned you."

"Her mother had questions about the dogs."

"I think we've kidded Matt enough," Mom said.

"Thanks, Mom."

"Did you like the new football magazine I put on your bed?" Dad asked. "I bought it because I know how much you like football."

"I thought you put it there. I really liked the article on the football players."

By the time Dad and I finished discussing football, I had five minutes before bedtime. I didn't want Mom to notice the time. Before I changed to my pajamas, I heard Mom call.

"Matt, are you in bed yet?"

There was the word I'd hoped to avoid for a while: bed. I wasn't sleepy.

"No," I replied. "I'm getting ready now."

Mom didn't have to say another word. I knew she would check on me later. For some reason, though, she didn't come in at all that night. That was different than what she normally did.

➤

Chapter

11

My friends and I joked around in the school hallway the next

day. When I overheard some jokes, I wondered if my friends

knew about my conversation with Cindy. I'd told no one. I didn't

think my parents had, either. Dad's kidding the night before had

embarrassed me. I didn't want anyone to know Cindy and I had

talked. Someone had found out, though. The kids' jokes made me

turn red as a tomato.

As my classmates entered our room, everyone hung up

their coats and put away their backpacks. Ms. Winthrop led us in

a couple of songs after she took attendance. For part of the morning, my teacher reviewed some information on England. Then, my classmates and I were to use the information to create an art project. During our art lesson, I didn't notice the golden retriever slink into the room. I had my head down, working on the art project. The kids' giggles from the front row caused me to look up. At first, my classmates appeared to be laughing at Cindy and me, but then the dog appeared. The dog walked to the back of the room, and it sat down. I didn't know whether Ms. Winthrop saw the dog or not, because she made no attempt to remove it.

My classmates and I kept working. Even though I wanted to touch the dog, I didn't. When I gazed at the dog, the retriever's eyes were on Ms. Winthrop.

My teacher pushed the room buzzer to call for someone to remove the dog. I volunteered to remove the dog, but the teacher didn't let me. I didn't expect any other answer. For a few minutes, I shared how Ben, Coach Brown, and I had found the dog in the woods. I was surprised when she questioned me about the dog.

"Is that your dog?"

"No. I'd like to adopt the dog, if no one claims it," I said.

"It's cruel to leave the dog without a master. Don't you think the retriever needs a home?" Ms. Winthrop asked.

I didn't tell her all the details, but I told her how people were trying to locate the dog's owner. I let Ms. Winthrop know how people were helping to care for the dog.

"I see why the dog is so friendly. She gets food and water from people she knows. The dog needs a permanent home, though."

"I know. I'm working on it," I said.

"That's good. I hope you find one soon, because the dog can't stay around school," Ms. Winthrop said.

"I'll keep trying. Coach Brown put an ad in the paper to locate the owner."

"That was a good idea. Has Coach Brown received any calls from the ad?"

"No, but some people are interested in the dog and its puppies. Dr. Thompson, a veterinarian in town, is taking care of all the retriever's puppies. A couple of puppies might have a home soon. Would you like one?"

"I can't take one, but Ms. Moore on the third grade hall might take a puppy. She wants one for her granddaughter. Check with her after school."

"I will. Thank you."

The school day continued without any other dog visits. At the end of the day, Ms. Winthrop let us write down names of people who might want a dog. The student with the most names would win thirty minutes of library time. I listed many names, since I wanted to win. The buzzing sound of Ms. Winthrop's timer caused me to set my pencil down. I passed my list in, and I waited for instructions.

Ms. Winthrop called me to her desk. I wanted to be a winner, but I wasn't sure why I was being called up front. Her explanation made me smile when she spoke to me.

"With your long list, I know you'll find someone to adopt all the dogs. You win thirty minutes in the library."

"That's a great prize! Thank you," I said.

"I know you're excited. Try to talk softly. We don't want to disturb other classes by talking loudly."

I nodded, and I took my seat. I smiled the rest of the day,

because of the prize I'd won.

During our restroom break, I asked Ms. Winthrop how to convince my parents to adopt the dog. I liked her idea.

"Maybe your parents would agree to let you take the dog until the owner is found," she said.

"There's one problem: my parents don't want the dog right now. We're going on a vacation soon."

"When are you going?"

"In a week."

"Would your parents let you keep the dog, if someone kept it while you were gone?"

"I'm not sure."

"Why don't you check with them tonight. Let me know by tomorrow. I might have a solution for you," Ms. Winthrop said.

"I will. Maybe I can find someone to adopt a puppy, too," I said.

"Don't forget to check with Ms. Moore."

"Thank you for reminding me," I replied.

The day continued without any other dog sightings. My

friends didn't kid me about Cindy again, either. I wanted the day to end; I needed to check on the dog.

I walked quickly down the hall when school ended. Before I walked very far, the principal, Mr. Henry, stopped me.

"Why are you going this way? Aren't you in Ms. Winthrop's class? Her class went out already."

"My teacher gave me permission to talk to Ms. Moore."

"You need a hall slip from your teacher. I need to know why students are going to different rooms," Mr. Henry said. "I'll let you go this time, but don't forget the hall pass in the future."

"I'll get one next time."

I walked ahead to Ms. Moore's room, tapping lightly on her door. I didn't know her too well, so I didn't want to upset her. When I saw the stacks of papers she had on her desk, I was glad to have Ms. Winthrop. My teacher didn't make us write all the time.

"What can I do for you?" Ms. Moore asked.

"Ms. Winthrop told me to see whether you'd like a puppy. Dr. Thompson, a veterinarian, has some puppies that need homes."

"What kind are they?" Ms. Moore asked.

"They are golden retriever puppies. Do you remember the big dog hanging around the school?"

"I saw the dogcatcher chasing a large golden dog. Is that the kind of dog you are talking about?"

"That's the one."

"How much are the puppies?"

"Dr. Thompson is only charging for the shots and food. I think he wants people to get them right away. Could you pick up a puppy today or tomorrow?"

"Oh, that might be a problem. Give me Dr. Thompson's number, so I can call him within the hour. I think I can work out something with him."

"Thank you, Ms. Moore. Please let me know if you adopt a dog. I'm trying to find homes for all of them."

"Oh, I'm sure things will work out, but I'll call you later," Ms. Moore said.

"Good-bye," I said. "Thanks."

I breathed a sign of relief, while I walked away. One less puppy needed a home now. I missed walking home with my friends, though. By the time I walked from Ms. Moore's classroom, I didn't see Ben or Jake. I ran ahead, trying to catch them. My friends weren't visible. I wanted to share my good news with them. I ran fast for five minutes, and I finally spotted Jake.

"Wait," I called out.

Jake kept walking. I tried again to get his attention.

"Jake, stop!" I screamed.

This time Jake heard me. He stopped and waited. By the time I caught up with him, I was out of breath. I said nothing as we walked along. Jake broke the silence after a few minutes.

"I waited for you at the corner of the building. The teacher on duty didn't want me to wait any longer, so I walked on."

"I have great news. Ms. Moore plans to take one of the puppies. Several people have promised to rescue them. I believe most of the dogs will have a home."

"What about the grown dog?"

"I want it. Ms. Winthrop is willing to care for the large dog during my family's vacation."

"Maybe your parents will change their minds," Jake said. "I don't mean to change the subject so quickly, but are we practicing archery later?"

"I'd like to practice. Call me after I get home. I'll check with Mom. I need to finish my homework," I said, as we parted.

"Hurry to finish everything. I'll call you in fifty-five minutes. You should be ready by then."

"I'll try my best," I said.

➤

Chapter

12

Before completing my homework and chores, I called a lady

who'd asked about adopting one of the dogs. She had decided

she didn't want one. I hoped the girls in my classroom, who'd

shown an interest in a puppy, didn't change their minds. I didn't

need to have to keep calling people. I needed the time on my

homework.

My clock showed that I had fifty minutes before archery

practice. I pulled the name list I'd made from my backpack.

When I started dialing numbers, Mom reminded me of my

homework. I needed Mom's permission to make the calls to

avoid trouble.

"Could I please make some phone calls about the dogs, Mom? I promise I'll do my homework later."

"You may make a few calls, but finish your homework before practice today."

When I grabbed my phone, I glanced outside my window. Seeing the wind jiggle my old swing, hanging from a magnolia tree, made me think of the good times I'd spent there. I hadn't used the swing in ages. Glancing at it again made me want to swing. A year ago, I'd swung often. Now I had no time for it, because of homework and practices. I had to stop daydreaming, so I didn't waste time. The phone calls had to be made about the dogs. Even though I gave my best dog adoption pitch to Ms. Read, she didn't want a dog.

I called four more people. None of them wanted a dog, either. For the next thirty minutes, I heard various excuses for not taking a dog. I wondered if people cared about dogs.

As I punched in the next phone number, Mom called me again. *What did she want this time?* At that moment, I remembered my homework. I turned off the phone before punching in another number. I called to Mom before she called me again.

"Mom, I need to make five more calls. May I do it now?" I begged.

"I thought you'd finished your calls."

"I've called five people. No one wants a dog."

"Call two more people. You need to get your homework. Try calling other people later."

On the next number I punched in, I received no answer. The grown retriever still didn't have a home. I didn't want anyone to adopt the grown dog; I wanted it. While I thought about the adoptions, something else came to mind: *I had to share my teacher's idea with Mom.* Homework had to be finished first.

I breezed through the math homework, which surprised me. Math usually took more time than other subjects, because of the number of problems assigned. The twelve questions in social studies were taking me longer than I'd expected. The last two questions were discussion ones. When the phone rang, Mom answered it. Before I could finish social studies, she called me.

"Matt, pick up the phone. Jake's calling you," Mom said.

"Hello," I answered.

"Are you ready for archery practice?"

"Just a minute. Let me check with Mom."

When I called Mom, she didn't answer me at first, so I went to look for her. I searched several rooms before I found her sorting laundry.

"Mom, Jake and I need to practice for the archery competition. Will you let me practice with him in fifteen minutes?"

"Is your homework finished?"

There was that word again: homework.

"No, Mom, but it shouldn't take more than thirty minutes to finish. I've finished math. There are only a couple of questions left in social studies to complete. I should have most of the work done in thirty minutes. Won't you let me finish later?"

"If your homework is complete in thirty minutes, you may go; if it's not, you may not."

Mom didn't understand. Jake was ready to leave now. I had to get my homework, so I had a problem. I phoned Jake.

"I want to leave, but Mom says I have to finish my

homework," I said. "Will you wait for me?"

"Why does your mom insist on you finishing your homework before practice?"

"She wants me to have good grades for getting into college. If I wait to finish my homework until after practice, she's afraid I'll fall asleep. She wants me to do my best."

"My mom wants me to get my homework, but she doesn't check it every day. As long as my grades are average, she doesn't care."

"You're lucky," I said. "I'd like to spend less time on homework. I have two questions to do. Could you practice a little later?"

"You have most of the work done. Why can't you finish the other two questions later?"

"No, I can't do that. I'll try to hurry, but I need thirty more minutes. The walk to school will take time, too. Have you looked at social studies?"

"No. Meet me at my house in thirty minutes. While I'm waiting for you, I'll work on my questions."

"All right. Thanks," I said.

I returned to my homework, but the phone rang again. However, I kept writing until I heard Mom's voice.

"The phone is for you. Jake is calling," Mom said.

I picked up the phone. "Are you ready?" he asked.

I was hoping Jake wasn't ready, since I had one question left. In another ten minutes, I thought I'd be through.

"Once you get here, I'll be ready to practice," Jake said.

I hung up the phone. By skimming the chapter material, I found the answer to the last question. I didn't have a chance to write it down, because the phone rang a third time. I tried to ignore it.

"Matt, Ms. Jones is calling you," Mom announced.

"I'll get it," I said.

By the time the conversation with Ms. Jones ended, I realized I had a problem. She wanted the mother dog. That dog was the one I wanted. My last homework question wasn't finished, but Jake was waiting on me. Mom would want to see my homework later. I decided to leave the homework paper in my book. With my best sprinting speed, I ran toward Jake's house.

On the way to Jake's, I wanted to think of a plan for keeping the older dog. *How would I talk my parents into keeping it?* Getting attached to the dog wasn't good, if Ms. Jones planned to adopt it. I hadn't been able to change my parents' minds so far.

By the time I arrived at Jake's house, I saw Ben and Jake standing in the driveway. Since Ben hadn't been involved in the archery practices in a couple of days, I was surprised to see him.

"Ben is practicing with us," Jake said.

"I didn't know you were still in the competition," I remarked.

"I was busy for a few days, but I'm competing," Ben said.

While the three of us walked to the school playground, we talked about the archery competition. We also discussed family vacation plans.

At archery practice, Coach Brown greeted us. Without wasting much time, he reminded us of the safety rules. Coach Brown practiced with the basketball players, but he kept an eye on us.

In the beginning of the practice, I had trouble. By the end of the practice, I had hit the bull's-eye.

"Look! I hit it!" I screamed.

"You don't have to brag," Ben replied.

"I didn't mean to brag, but I'm happy to be improving. I didn't start out well. Things seem to be turning around."

"It takes time to get warmed up," Jake said.

"You're right, Jake. I've got to go now," I said.

"Matt, don't you want to stay longer?" Ben asked.

"No. I've got to get home. We've practiced over an hour."

"Matt, you're afraid Jake and I might catch up." Ben said.

I shook my head from side to side. "I have to finish my homework. Mom thinks I'm finished. I have the last question to do. I still have one dog adoption to take care of."

"Oh, let's shoot a few more arrows," Jake said. "Your mom might forget the homework."

I stood there torn between my friends' and my mom's instructions. Finishing the last homework question shouldn't take long. I chose to stay with my friends.

Chapter

13

Without making a lot of noise, I entered the side door at home.
My last homework question needed completing. On tiptoes, I
slipped to my room. I opened my book, searching for the answer
to the question left undone. I didn't get finished before I heard
footsteps; they were loud, like they were outside my bedroom
door. Before I had time to write anything, my bedroom door flew
open. I prepared myself for an ugly scene while someone entered
behind me.

"I didn't hear you come in. How was your practice?" Dad
asked.

"It was fun, but I only hit the bull's-eye once. Last time I hit it twice."

"Well, that's pretty good. You can't expect to hit it every time. Some people struggle to hit it at all. What are you working on?"

Answering Dad's question might get me into trouble. He knew Mom's homework rule. I didn't want him to share my homework information with Mom. I tried to skip his question by telling about Jake's archery shot, but Dad repeated his question. I stared at the floor before speaking.

"I'm finishing my last question," I said.

"I thought you'd finished already."

"I did my math. My social studies homework is almost finished."

"I'll let you finish, because your mom will check it shortly."

"Thanks, Dad."

"Next time, finish it before you leave. You know the homework rule."

"I'm sorry, Dad. I'll do better. The phone calls I had to

make about the dogs took time. I received several other calls, too."

"If there's a problem getting your homework, drop the archery competition."

"I usually finish my homework before practice, Dad."

"I'll talk to you later," he said.

"Whew, that was close," I said to myself. "I hope Dad doesn't tell Mom."

I read the last question. It didn't take long to find the answer, and I wrote it down quickly. Right before Mom entered, I'd placed my homework in my backpack.

"Is your homework ready for me to check?"

"Yes, I'll get it."

I reopened my backpack, pulling the papers out for Mom. It didn't take long for her to check them over.

"Matt, your work looks fine. You might want to read until time for your television show," Mom said.

"Thanks, Mom. Will you call me when it's time?"

"I'll let you know."

After grabbing my book to read, I was no longer nervous.

Dad knew I had to finish my last homework question, but apparently he hadn't told Mom. From now on, I planned to finish my homework before practicing archery.

For a few minutes I read. I stopped when I remembered that I needed to make a phone call. I'd promised to call Ms. Jones about the grown golden retriever. I hesitated, because I was trying to come up with a plan to keep the dog. *Should I ask my parents another time about keeping the grown dog?* I knew I had to ask them.

When I walked to the kitchen for a snack, I found my parents in the family room. I knew it was risky to ask questions when they were together. Talking to one parent at the time was better. I had no choice, since I was under a time limit.

"I thought you were reading your book," Mom said.

"I read it for a while. In a few minutes, I have to call Ms. Jones. She wants to adopt the large dog, but I want it. Would you let me have the grown dog?"

"I don't think we want a dog that large. On the trip, we don't have room for it."

"Mom, please let me have the grown dog. My teacher

offered to get someone to keep it while we're gone. She's a great dog!"

"Your mom is right, Matt. A large dog is a lot of work. It would take more time to feed and care for it. Dogs need love and attention, too. Taking care of the dog would be your responsibility."

"I know, but today I have to call Ms. Jones. I don't want to give the dog away."

"Tell Ms. Jones to come get the dog. We can get a dog after the trip."

"I'll call her now." I said.

Before making the phone call, I looked out my bedroom window. In the center of the backyard, I saw the beautiful dog that I'd fed, petted, and loved. A new plea to keep the grown dog hadn't changed my parents' minds. My eyes misted over. During the time I cried, no one heard me. The television blotted out my sobs.

When I stopped crying, I washed my face and wiped the tears. I telephoned Ms. Jones. Her phone rang three times before anyone answered it.

"Hello," Ms. Jones said.

"This is Matt. I'm the boy who called you about the dog. Are you still planning to get it?" I asked.

"I want the mother dog."

With a lump in my throat, I asked, "When do you plan to get it?"

"Tomorrow afternoon around four o'clock. Will that time work for you?"

"I'll have the dog ready," I said. "Ms. Jones, you can pick it up from 2010 Highway 54."

"That sounds great. Tell me the price for the dog again."

"You will only have to pay for the dog's shots," I said. "I'll have the information when you come."

"I'll be there tomorrow afternoon at four o'clock."

I didn't know what to do next. I set the phone down, but I grabbed it again to call Jake. When I punched in Jake's phone number, Mom appeared. Jake hadn't answered yet, so I turned off the phone.

"It's time for your television show," Mom said.

"I'll pass on it tonight," I replied.

"That's the first time that's happened. Matt, you're not sick, are you? Who are you calling?"

"I'm calling Jake. I'm not sick."

"Oh, I'm sorry we can't get the dog. I know how much you want it," Mom said. "Perhaps, we'll get a dog when we return."

"No dog will be like that one, though."

"I know you're upset now, but things will get better. Matt, what do you plan to do during television time?"

"After I call Jake, I plan to read again."

"Are you going to be all right, Matt?"

I nodded my head up and down while brushing the tears away. When my mom left the room, I called Jake. His phone rang six times before his mother's voice came on the line.

"May I speak to Jake?" I asked.

"Wait a minute. I'll get him," Mrs. Graham responded.

I waited a long time before Jake answered. When he spoke, I knew he understood my feelings. Jake had become attached to the mother dog like me.

"Jake, Ms. Jones plans to take the dog tomorrow. Will

you help me with it?" I asked.

"I don't think we'll have a problem with the dog. It'll probably follow us," Jake said.

"I'll have a leash to attach to its collar," I said.

"I guess your parents didn't want the dog."

I cleared my throat, trying to make it sound like I was hoarse. I paused before speaking. I didn't want Jake to know I'd been crying.

"No, they didn't want it," I replied.

"That's too bad. You'd think our parents would want a good dog."

"I might get a dog after our vacation," I said.

"You might like a puppy better. They are real playful. My parents don't want any dog," Jake said.

"I'd take a puppy, but I like the big dog best."

"I'll help you after school. My homework's not finished, so I have to go now. My mom wants me in bed early tonight."

"I'll see you tomorrow," I said.

Oh, if only I could get my parents to change their minds about the grown dog.

Chapter

14

The strong wind caused me to shiver, while I walked to Jake's house. I dreaded the afternoon, because I didn't want to give the grown dog away. At Jake's house, the howling winds blew fiercely. I set my backpack down. Then, I buttoned my coat, trying to keep warm in the gusty wind. I didn't wait long until Jake appeared.

"I hope it's not so windy this afternoon," I said.

While I stood next to Jake, he shook a bit from the wind; and he zipped his coat. He threw his hat on his head, covering it from the wind. His gloves, stored inside his coat pockets, came out to cover his fingers.

"Man, it's cold this morning," Jake said, shivering. "Why are you worried about this afternoon?"

"Don't tell me you've forgotten."

Jake looked puzzled at first. He didn't seem to recall what I'd asked him to do in the afternoon. His puzzled look changed when he realized what we had to do.

"We have to get the dog ready for Ms. Jones, don't we? I hope it warms up this afternoon."

I clenched my jaw before speaking. Without crying, I managed to answer his question. "Yes, Ms. Jones is getting the dog today."

"At least, the dog will have a home. I will miss her," Jake said.

I turned my head away, so Jake wouldn't notice how sad I was. A tear filled one of my eyes. With one arm, I wiped it away on my coat sleeve.

"I wish my family would go on vacation now, so I wouldn't have as much time to think about the dog," I said.

"Matt, you'll have fun on your vacation. Think of the

new things to see and do. The vacation might make you forget about the dog."

"If I could choose the dog or the vacation, I'd choose the dog."

"*Would* you choose the dog?" Jake asked.

"Yes, wouldn't you?"

"I'm not sure I would," Jake said.

On our arrival at school, the teacher on duty was telling students to be quiet in the halls. We closed our mouths to avoid getting into trouble.

During the morning activities, I daydreamed. The afternoon task of moving the dog was one I wanted to put off. I didn't participate in the class discussions, like I usually did.

The school day dragged by with the written and oral work. I kept hoping my parents would change their minds about the retriever. After the bell rang, Jake and I explained our plans to the teacher. We needed her permission to search the school grounds for the dog.

"Let me check with your parents. It will only take a few minutes," Ms. Winthrop said.

Once our parents agreed for us to get the dog, we searched the school grounds. At first, we didn't see the dog, but then it rushed from the woods with a wagging tail.

When the dog came close to us, we petted it. I attached the leash to its collar, and Jake continued to pet the dog. As it walked along, the dog pulled on the leash. Jake and I used commands to stop it. When the dog obeyed us, I gave it treats.

After Jake and I walked the dog home, we played fetch with it in the backyard. Once it dropped down to rest, Jake and I hooked the gate and left the dog. We walked to the front yard and played. When the dog started barking, we tried to ignore its bark. Mom didn't ignore the dog's bark; she called to me.

"Matt, it's time to do your homework. I see the dog is ready for Ms. Jones. She should be here soon."

I hated to tell Jake good-bye. He was the only one I opened up to about the dog. As Jake started to leave, we agreed on our practice time for the next day. The archery tournament date was drawing near, so I wanted to practice every day.

I knew Jake liked the dog as much as I did, so I suggested taking a few minutes to pet it together. Once we started to open the gate, our plans ended abruptly. My mom appeared.

"Aren't you coming in, Matt?" Mom asked.

"Mom, I'm on my way. We just wanted to pet the dog one last time," I said.

"Hurry up. Homework and dinner need to be finished. Ms. Jones will be here soon. You'll have to spend time telling her about the dog. I don't want you to stay up too late."

"Jake and I will hurry to pet the dog," I assured Mom.

Before we left the golden retriever, Jake and I threw the ball for the dog to fetch. It brought the ball to me; and we hugged and praised the dog. When Jake and I started to leave, we gave it a treat.

I stepped into my room after Jake left. I pulled my homework from my backpack. As I stared at the assignment list, I realized I'd forgotten the social studies test tomorrow. Right then, I knew my homework would take longer than it usually did.

I wanted to finish my homework before Ms. Jones arrived. While I studied, I thought of a new plan. *If I'd spend extra time with Ms. Jones, I would have the dog for a longer period of time. Ms. Jones might change her mind about the dog.*

The dog hadn't ever been mine, but I felt like the owner. I liked having the dog follow me home. I had fun playing the fetch games with it, too.

When I finished studying for the test, I reached for my reading assignment. It was short. I thought it wouldn't take me too long to finish. I liked reading, but I wanted to choose my own books. Before long, I'd read the textbook material, cleaned my desk, and packed my backpack.

At the dinner table, Mom asked me about my homework. I was happy to tell her I'd finished everything. I didn't have much to tell about school. During the evening meal, my parents avoided discussing the dog. They discussed the vacation plans with me. When the doorbell rang, interrupting our dinner, it was Ms. Jones. I walked slowly to the door.

Once introductions were made, I took Ms. Jones to the backyard. I wanted her to see the dog, while Dad followed along. I hoped she wouldn't want such a large dog. But, of course, I knew better. I really figured anyone would like the dog.

Ms. Jones agreed to take the dog, and then I shared dog stories with her. When I'd talked to Ms. Jones as long as possible, I helped get the dog inside the car.

I watched the car pull away with the golden retriever's head out. It was looking back at me. I ran down the sidewalk, watching the dog disappear. I could do nothing. I knew I'd loss the dog of my dreams. When Mom came out to get me, I raced inside to finish my evening meal. My appetite was gone. Losing the dog made me sob again. My mom tried to comfort me.

"Matt, after you finish eating, you might want to read. It will be bedtime soon."

I ate a couple of bites, but then hurried to my room. I punched in Jake's number to tell him about Ms. Jones's visit. I didn't talk to him for very long before I started weeping. My heart was no longer into the archery competition as much. I thought of only one thing: *the golden dog.*

➤

Chapter

15

On Saturday, Jake, Ben, and I walked toward the school for the archery competition practice. No whimpering sounds came from the woods behind the school. My friends and I practiced shooting for a while. Each one of us tried to make a bull's-eye. When we took a break, I heard a noise coming from the woods. I knew one thing for sure: the golden retriever had a new owner. The noise couldn't have been from the dog found in the woods. By now, I figured the dog had settled in its new yard. I set my bow and arrow down, dashing into the woods.

"Matt, come back. We might get into trouble," Jake said.

"I'll be okay. I'll only be a minute."

"Wait for an adult to go with us," Ben remarked.

I tuned my friends' words out, darting ahead. I didn't want the coach to see me. When I turned around, no one had followed me. Suddenly, a voice rang out in the distance.

"Matt, where are you?"

I recognized Coach Brown's voice, so I hurried to get back to the playground. As I stepped from the woods, a loud noise caused my heart to start racing. At first, there was nothing there when I turned around. My friends grinned as I stood before them. I turned around again to see why my friends were grinning. At that moment, a golden retriever approached me, sniffing everything in sight. The dog looked the same color as the one I'd given Ms. Jones.

"Well, I see the dog's followed you," Coach Brown said. "It looks like it's escaped."

"Are you sure this dog is the one I gave away?" I asked.

Jake smiled and nodded. "I'm sure it is."

"Yes," Ben said. "See the dark shoulder spots. It has the same white markings on the face, belly, and tail, as the dog we found."

"Let me look," the coach said, bending down to examine the dog.

"Yesterday I talked to Ms. Jones. She adopted the dog. I saw Ms. Jones drive away with the dog," I replied.

"Dogs will follow people for miles. That dog thinks you're its master," Coach Brown said.

"I want it to be, but Mom and Dad don't want the grown dog. My parents said that we might get one after vacation. I'll call Ms. Jones to come get it."

"Ms. Jones might not want the dog now. The retriever ran away," Jake said.

"If Ms. Jones doesn't want it, we're back to square one," Coach Brown said. "Matt will have to find the dog a new owner."

"I think I can feed the dog while your family goes on vacation," Jake suggested.

"Matt needs to contact Ms. Jones, so the dog can be returned. She is the owner," Coach Brown said.

When my friends and I left the playground, the golden

retriever followed us. At home, I placed it into the family's fenced backyard until I could reach Ms. Jones. Before I explained anything to my parents, Mom asked me why the dog was in our backyard. I sat down with Mom in the kitchen, and I told her the whole story. Once Mom and I finished talking, I punched in Ms. Jones's number. She answered after three rings.

"Hello," Ms. Jones said."

I told Ms. Jones who I was; and I told her why I had her dog.

"I guess the dog found a way out. It probably crawled under where there's a gap between the fence and ground. My husband can repair it after he gets home. I can pick the dog up at seven o'clock tonight. Is that okay?" Ms. Jones asked.

I explained to Ms. Jones that I needed to discuss the time she'd mentioned with Mom. She agreed to wait on the phone for me.

"Is it okay for Ms. Jones to come tonight at seven o'clock?" I asked.

Mom looked at her watch. "That will be fine, but I hope Ms. Jones can find a way to keep the dog in her yard."

Once I finished the conversation, I saw Mom smile. I didn't bother to ask her what was funny.

Giving up the dog was hard the first time. I didn't want to think about losing it again.

I had trouble concentrating on anything after Ms. Jones took the dog. Even though it was hard to part with the retriever, I wanted the dog to be happy.

➤

Chapter

16

The next day, Ms. Winthrop called on me in math. I didn't
answer. Participating in the lesson wasn't as much fun without
the dog in the classroom. During the lesson, I wasn't listening
closely. My mind was on the dog. I wanted it to be mine. I knew
Ms. Jones thought she'd secured the dog in her yard before, but
she hadn't.

Once the school day ended, Ben and I walked along our
usual path. Jake wasn't with us. I missed him, but Jake was
resting at home with a fever. While Ben and I strolled home, we
discussed our upcoming baseball game. Our conversation blotted

out everything around us. Suddenly, a distant bark caused me to stop.

"Did you hear that?" I asked Ben.

"No," Ben said. "I think I know what made the noise."

At that moment, the golden retriever edged right behind me. "Hi," I said, while I stroked her fur.

"That dog thinks you're its master," Ben said. "Everywhere you go, it follows."

"The dog follows you like it does me. Did you ask your mom about keeping it?"

"My mom said, 'We don't need a dog to look after,' so I can't take it."

"I've asked my parents more than once. They keep saying they don't want a dog now," I said.

"Why not now? The dog's easy to care for."

"My parents don't want the dog because of our vacation coming up. Ms. Winthrop offered to find a pet sitter during our vacation. She knew how much I wanted the dog. I couldn't change my parents' minds, though."

Since the dog kept following us, Ben came home with

me. He helped me put the dog inside my family's fenced area. We played a game of fetch with the dog for a little while, and then we left the dog. I forgot to tell Mom that the dog followed us home.

Ben and I made plans to practice archery and baseball later. Before we made final plans, he had to call his mother. I whipped out my homework to work on, while he was on the phone. I had to complete it before I left for our practices.

I looked forward to having a friend over. Having someone to walk to practice with me would be fun, too. Not having my homework finished made me nervous. I could tell by Ben's tapping foot that he was ready to practice now, but I wasn't. I explained to him how I had to finish my homework before practice, so Ben worked on his homework beside me.

Before Ben and I left for our after-school activities, Mom gave us each a snack: an apple. Both of us practically inhaled our apples. Once I finished my homework, little time remained to get to our archery practice and baseball tryout. We ran as fast as possible for a while, but then we slowed down.

On the way, I hummed a tune while Ben joined in. I tried

harmonizing with him to make the song more interesting.

"Why didn't you tell me you like to sing? Perhaps I could play my harmonica while you sing," Ben suggested.

"I just sing when I'm happy, like when my homework's finished," I said.

"I know. I like to get mine finished, but I tend to put it off."

Before long we were at school. Ben and I set up the archery equipment quickly. We practiced for a little over an hour. At first, our arrows landed close to the target. As our practice continued, both of us did worse. I wanted to make a bull's-eye that day, but it didn't happen.

During our baseball tryout session, Ben and I did better than at archery practice. I slugged the ball and hit a home run. After I hit the ball into the outfield, my insides became as pudding. I ran quickly around the bases. I wanted to be on the school team.

Ben played baseball so well that I thought he'd make the team. He had two home runs. When Coach Brown called us to read the team members' names, I crossed my fingers. His list took several minutes to read. After the coach reached the end of the list, he called my name and Ben's. I was the next to last name called, but it didn't matter. I'd made the team.

At the end of the tryouts, Ben and I walked home. We discussed our team's stats. While we walked, the sky darkened; so, once we reached Ben's house, I didn't linger.

"Good-bye," I said.

I hurried home before the storm hit. When I reached my house, a barking noise greeted me. I didn't stop to pet the dog, because I needed to call Ms. Jones. I rushed into my room, and I punched in her number. No one answered Ms. Jones's phone. I didn't know what to do.

I knew the dog must be hungry, so I fed it. Without spilling any water, I filled the dog's water bowl up, too. As I started out the fence, the dog ran toward me. To keep it from escaping, I threw a ball in the yard, distracting the dog. While the retriever ran for it, I slipped out.

As I closed the gate, a few raindrops fell. I hurried to call Ms. Jones again. I didn't want my parents to think I was trying to keep the dog. Once someone answered Ms. Jones's phone, I didn't recognize the voice.

"Hello, this is Ms. Jones's residence. Could I take a message for you?"

I explained why I'd called, so Ms. Jones came to the phone. After Ms. Jones came on the line, I became tongue-tied, trying to explain the problem. I was surprised at Ms. Jones's response.

"Maybe you should keep the dog," she said. "It is always going to your house."

"But, it's your dog, not mine," I said.

"You like the dog, don't you, Matt? I'm willing to let you have it back."

"I like the dog a lot. There's a problem, though. My parents probably won't let me keep it."

"If you want to ask them about the dog, I'll wait on the line."

Before asking my parents, I said, "Give me a minute, please."

After searching for Mom, I found her in her room crocheting. I wanted to say the right thing, so I paused before speaking.

"Mom, Ms. Jones asked if we could keep the dog. She's upset because the dog keeps running away. She's willing to give it back to us."

I stood there for what seemed like an hour, waiting for Mom to speak. Mom finally broke her silence.

"I'll discuss the situation with your father. Ask Ms. Jones whether we can talk to her tomorrow. We'll keep the dog overnight, so Ms. Jones won't have to come out in the storm."

"Thanks, Mom."

"Don't get your hopes up too high," Mom said.

I rushed back to the phone to tell Ms. Jones what Mom had said. By the time I'd hung up, I had started planning how to win Dad over. I had to persuade him to keep the dog. If I could say the right words, Dad might change his mind. Mom's expression had changed when I'd mentioned keeping the dog. She didn't look as serious as she'd looked before. In the past, Mom had not wanted the dog at all. But today, Mom had patted me on the shoulder. She'd smiled, too.

➤

Chapter

17

Once Dad arrived from work, I had to discuss keeping the grown

dog with him. I tried not to mention it right away. When I'd

spoken to Dad right after work on other days, he'd shooed me

away. I sat in the room with Dad reading from my library book. I

planned to ask my question after Dad had relaxed.

While peering from the corner of my eyes, I caught Dad

looking over his mail. Then, my parents chatted before Mom

made dinner. I watched as Dad grabbed his newspaper. When he

sat in his favorite chair, I knew it was time to move near him. I

kept reading my book while Dad read the newspaper. Once Dad

set his newspaper aside, it seemed like the perfect time for asking my question. I needed an answer for Ms. Jones that evening, so I set my book down. I was ready to ask Dad my question.

"Dad, you know the dog I gave away . . .?"

"What about it?" Dad interrupted.

"Well, there's a problem with the dog."

"What's wrong? I thought Ms. Jones adopted the dog."

"Yes, but it escaped," I said.

"Didn't Ms. Jones pick the dog up?"

"She did, but it ran away again."

"So, is Ms. Jones coming to get the dog this evening?"

"Ms. Jones wants me to take the dog back."

"I thought she liked the dog," Dad said. "Why doesn't she want the dog?"

"She told me, 'I think the retriever sees you as its master.' "

"Why does Ms. Jones think that?"

"For two days in a row, the dog followed me home."

"Doesn't Ms. Jones have a fenced yard?"

"She does but the dog gets out."

"The dog doesn't dig much here. Is it digging out over there?" Dad asked. "It sounds like you need to find another home for it."

Dad's answer wasn't the one I wanted to hear. I wanted to keep the grown dog.

"What will I do with it now?" I asked.

"The dog can stay a week. It will have to go to the Humane Society after that. We're not keeping it."

I couldn't give up that easily, so I began again, "But Dad . . ."

"The subject is closed. Do you understand me?"

"Yes," I said.

I left the room with weeping eyes, and I bit my lip. Giving the dog away broke my heart; it was terrible. My reading and television time would be delayed tonight, because I had to find another home for the grown dog. I reached for my list from my desk. By the time I'd punched in ten numbers, no one had agreed to take the grown dog. When I checked my name list, I'd called all the names I had.

To get more phone numbers to call, I punched in Ben's

number. He had few new suggestions, so I called Jake. He wasn't at home. I telephoned other friends, but no one added to my list. I tossed my list on my desk, but then it occurred to me to call Lynn. She loved dogs. I thought she might know someone who wanted a dog.

By the time I'd reached for the phone again, I'd lost my nerve to call Lynn. I didn't like calling girls. They were so different than boys; girls tended to think a boy was their boyfriend, if a boy spoke to them. I didn't need a girl to think that, because I wasn't interested in a girlfriend. The grown dog needed a home, though. I stood there a minute, trying to think of what to say to Lynn. Nothing came to mind, so I reached for a pen and paper. I decided to write the words I'd say ahead of time. If I stumbled over the words, I'd have a prompt to help me.

With my paper and pen set beside me, I punched in Lynn's number. The moment Lynn's mother answered, I wanted to hang up. I didn't; instead, I took a deep breath, and I asked for Lynn.

While I waited for Lynn, it seemed like an eternity. The minute hand showed it actually had been only two minutes.

"Hello," Lynn said.

"Lynn, do you know anyone who wants the golden retriever we found at school?" I asked.

"I thought the dog had an owner," Lynn said.

"Ms. Jones took her for two days, but she's changed her mind about the dog."

"I would think she'd love that dog. Matt, if you'll wait a minute, I'll ask my mom for some people's names."

"I'll wait," I said, shifting from one foot to the other.

I waited for Lynn to return. She was able to give me five new names and phone numbers to call.

"Will you wait for me to write them down?" I asked.

"I'll try, but hurry. I have to practice the flute for an hour."

I snatched my pen and wrote fast. Even though I didn't know how to spell all the names, I wrote them down like they sounded. Beside each name, I wrote their phone number. When I'd finished, I thanked Lynn for her help.

It took me an hour to call the five people on my list, but no one wanted a dog. As I sat there, my head nodded and my eyes closed.

When I awakened again, I looked at my multiple lists. I still needed more names. One classmate I thought of calling was Cindy. I really didn't want to call another girl, but I called her anyway. When she answered, I had trouble talking, because I was tired. I'd called so many people already. I waited patiently for her to give me new information.

"I might have a couple of names for you," Cindy replied.

I jotted down the names. When I'd finished, I thanked Cindy. Right away, I called the numbers she'd given me. One family wanted the grown dog, but had no place to keep it. I had no more time that night for calling people. The clock hands indicated it was my bedtime.

As soon as Mom announced it, I grabbed my library book. I put my head on my pillow to read my book. Before long, I dreamed that a monster was trying to get me.

"Help, help!" I screamed from a deep sleep.

When Mom appeared, I shared my bad dream with her. Once we were too tired to talk any longer, I turned over and slept.

➤

Chapter

18

The curtain in my bedroom hung with a slight opening in the middle. For days, I'd pulled it apart, watching the huge dog in the yard. Today was no exception. I pulled the curtain aside, trying to catch a glimpse of the dog. It was still too dark outside. I padded to the hallway to turn on the outside lights. When the backyard lights came on, the golden retriever barked.

I turned off the light switch to stop the dog's piercing yelp. I didn't do it fast enough. I heard footsteps in the hallway. Right before Dad entered my room, I ran to my bed; I pulled up the covers.

"Why were you up? Did the dog wake you?" Dad asked.

Dad's tousled hair and light beard caused me to pause before speaking. Irritating him before he was fully awake wasn't something I wanted to do. If I said the wrong thing, he might be a little cross. I knew Dad hadn't had his coffee yet, so I needed to be careful what I said. I didn't want to tell him what I'd done, but I did.

Once Dad returned to his room, I reached for my book. I fell asleep with the book in my hands. When I awoke a second time, there was no noise in the entire house. I thought my parents were asleep.

I crept to my parents' bedroom door. My hand tapped lightly on it. No one answered, so I knocked again. No sounds came from their room. I opened the door to Dad's loud snores. *A day off from school would be fun.* I decided that plan might not work. My parents wanted me in school every day. I didn't want makeup work to do, either.

I slipped to Mom's side of the bed to wake her. My stomach was growling; I needed some breakfast. I shook Mom gently.

"Good morning," I said.

"What time is it?" Mom said, squinting.

"It's eight o'clock."

"Oh, no. You're going to be late! I'll fix you some cereal and fruit. You get dressed. I'll drive you to school," Mom said, jumping up.

"Mom, I'll need a written excuse for being late."

"Bring me some paper and a pen. Hurry!"

I brought Mom the paper and pen she needed. In five minutes, my clothes were on; in two minutes, I'd washed my face. I rushed to eat my cereal. Mom and I said little during breakfast, since Mom was jotting down my note.

Mom sent me to the garage to put my backpack in the car. During the time I waited for Mom, I checked on the dog. The dog nuzzled her nose against me through the fence. I didn't want to leave the retriever. While Mom finished dressing, I put the dog in the car. I planned to take it to the wooded area at school. I intended to get the dog in the afternoon.

When Mom darted out the kitchen door, I opened and closed the car door. I had to run back inside to get my lunch money. I'd left it on my desk. Once I returned, Mom wasn't smiling like she usually did, so I knew I was in trouble. I'd forgotten about the dog being in the car. Once I opened the car door, the dog's nose was resting between the two front seats. Then Mom began questioning me.

"Why aren't you in the car? You were ready fifteen minutes ago. What was so important that you had to go back for?" Mom asked.

I explained how I'd forgotten my lunch money. I didn't say anything about the dog, hoping she wouldn't ask about it.

"And why is the dog in the car? Is someone picking it up from school? It doesn't belong here."

"Could we leave the dog inside the car now? "I need to get to school," I said.

Mom agreed that I needed to leave right then. During our drive to school, I told Mom about my plans for the dog. I waited for her comments, but she didn't say anything for a while. I assumed she didn't object, but I was wrong.

"The dog might get hurt in the woods at school. It could injure some child on the playground," Mom said. "It needs a safe, large area to roam."

"Mom, the dog has lived in the woods for a while," I said.

"I know, but that's not a good place for it. You're already late. Taking the dog to the woods will make you later. You might get into trouble."

"I'm not worried. I've taken care of the dog in the woods before."

"I don't like it, but I guess we have no other choice now. I'll wait here. Before you enter the building, come back around front. I want to see you enter the building," Mom said.

I knew Mom didn't want me to leave the dog behind the school, but she hadn't handled the dog like I had. I was glad Mom had agreed to be there for me.

Once I'd left the dog in the woods, I waved to Mom. I started inside the school, but Mom motioned me toward the car.

"Don't forget the dog this afternoon. I don't want you and Dad having to get the dog later. I'll pick you up after school." Mom said.

"I'll have the dog ready. Mom, will I be able to practice

baseball today?" I asked.

"I guess so. You have a lot of outside activities. I don't want your grades slipping, because you don't have enough study time."

While I waved good-bye to Mom, I didn't understand why she expected all *A*'s and *B*'s. My friends' moms didn't push grades so much. Most of their report cards had average grades on them. They didn't get restricted unless they had failing grades. I got restricted for a week, if I made below a *B* on anything.

➤

Chapter

19

On my way to class, I stopped by the office to get a late entrance slip. I needed one to give to my teacher. When I gave Ms. Winthrop my yellow office slip, she looked surprised to see me; I was never late.

I barely had time to put my supplies away. Before I started on my work, the teacher called my reading group. She assigned us a story and some questions. While my group worked in the reading area, another group worked on assignments in a different area. A third group used computer programs. Classmates who had completed their work were allowed to read for pleasure. The day seemed like other days until classmates started giggling. When the teacher questioned Cindy about the giggling, she paused before answering. The teacher's stern look and voice caused everyone to stop giggling right then.

"I hope you're working on your assignments. The class will not go outside today, if assignments aren't completed," Ms. Winthrop said.

My classmates returned to their work. During my reading group, I saw the grown dog walk down a classroom aisle. I slid my feet under my chair as it came near. The dog sat beside me. The rest of the reading time, I didn't move or say a word.

"I guess the dog plans to read with us," Ms. Winthrop said, smiling. "It can't stay. I'll call the office for help to remove it."

While other students laughed, I kept reading. I checked to see where the dog was a couple of times. It didn't leave my side. Even though the dog nudged me once, I ignored it. I didn't say anything, because I didn't want to get into trouble.

Once my group went to their seats, I saw Ms. Winthrop press the office call button. I knew the call to the head custodian,

Mr. Bentley, meant that the dog was being removed. Ms. Winthrop's words made me sad.

"The custodian needs to remove a dog from my classroom," she said.

While the class waited for Mr. Bentley to arrive, I continued working. The dog looked like it was reading from my book for a few seconds.

Mr. Bentley smiled as he entered the room. When he found the dog sitting beside me, he walked over to Ms. Winthrop. He whispered something to her. In a flash, Mr. Bentley left the room. I didn't know why he hadn't taken the dog out. It was fine with me, though.

No sooner did Mr. Bentley disappear than he reappeared. He held a leash in his hands. Mr. Bentley struggled to get the dog to move, but he finally did.

Several days before, I'd watched the dogcatcher try to use a leash. The leash hadn't worked; instead, the dog had escaped. I wanted to help the grown dog this time, but I didn't know how.

Group reading instruction continued. The teacher said nothing about the dog. Even though my group went to their seats to complete assignments, I had more important things to do. I wanted to locate where the dog was. So, I raised my hand, and I asked to go to the restroom.

"You may be excused, but hurry back," Ms. Winthrop said. "We'll begin the math test shortly. Don't hold the class up. I know everyone wants to go outside on time."

Ms. Winthrop's words made me sprint out the door, because I didn't want to miss playing our game. I liked exercising, talking, and playing with my friends.

When I walked into the hall, I looked around. The dog wasn't in sight. A slight whimpering cry caught my attention, though. I knew the sound must be close to where I was standing. The whimpering sound increased when I stood beside the janitor's closet. The closet door stood ajar, which was different than normal. Once I made sure that no one was around, I opened the closet. I discovered a large cage with the dog inside. I didn't stop to think about the trouble I was causing, as I let the dog out.

When the dog left the cage, it ran out the back door. I chased the dog, but the retriever ran fast. Right before it disappeared into the woods, I caught a glimpse of its tail. I knew it was safer in the woods, so I didn't chase it. I ran into the restroom.

As I entered the restroom, heavy footsteps echoed in the hallway. I rushed to a restroom stall; I didn't want Mr. Bentley to recognize me in the hall. He might figure out that I had something to do with the dog's escape. I waited in the restroom to avoid contact with him. Once the footsteps faded, I scrambled to my seat in the room. I listened to Ms. Winthrop give us the test instructions. And then, I started on my test. I turned in my paper when I'd finished doing my best. I knew I needed to do well in school, if I wanted to continue my after-school activities.

While I waited for my classmates to finish, my thoughts returned to the dog. My class would be outside soon, but I wouldn't be able to check on the dog until later. *I had to be careful. No one must know that I let the dog out.* I had another problem: I had to get the dog without anyone seeing me after school. I didn't want to create a problem for Mom or me. I needed Mom on my side.

In the afternoon, the class went outside to play baseball. It was fun to play with my friends. When we had to go inside, my team had the most runs.

Soon the bell sounded, so I grabbed my backpack. I rushed up the hallway and out the door. Ben and Jake met me outside. At first, they kidded me about the dog.

While we stood in front of the school, I talked quietly to my friends. I didn't want to get the dog until most of the teachers left their duty. I wanted no one to see me. I didn't discuss the dog with my friends for quite a while.

"The dog is in the woods. Mom is waiting for me to put it in the car. Maybe we can get together for archery and baseball practices later," I said.

"Do you need for us to help you?" Ben asked.

"No. I'll get the dog."

"Hey, I thought Mr. Bentley had the dogcatcher take it away," Jake said.

"Don't talk so loudly. I have to go now. I'll fill you in later."

I saw Mom's car several yards from the school entrance, so I slipped to the back of the school building. With care, I crept into the woods to get the dog.

When I first called the dog, it didn't come. I strolled into the woods to look for it. Before I'd gone far, I heard a familiar voice behind me.

"What are you doing back here? You know the rules," Coach Brown said.

I didn't want to share what had happened earlier today with Coach Brown. He might get upset with me. I didn't know whether he knew the dog was on the loose or not, so I paused before speaking.

"Answer my question, Matt."

"Mom brought me to school. I was running late today."

Coach Brown interrupted. "I thought Ms. Jones adopted the dog. What happened? When the dog showed up again at school, I heard that Mr. Bentley caught it. He put the dog in his storage closet."

I knew Coach Brown hadn't witnessed me helping the dog escape. I'd unlatched the cage without anyone around. Even though there wasn't much time, I had to tell the coach why I was there. Mom was out front, so I had to hurry.

I stood there trembling, with my stomach flipping like

flapjacks. I managed to tell Coach Brown how I'd left the dog in the woods that morning. I left out the part about me setting the dog free from the cage, though.

"So, you're back here to get the dog," Coach Brown remarked.

"Yes," I said, trying to avoid saying anymore.

"That still doesn't explain how the dog escaped," Coach Brown said.

"Please help me find the dog. Mom wants me to take it home. Ms. Jones doesn't want the dog. Mom and I are going to find another home for it."

"I'll help, but keep the dog away from the school. The dogcatcher will get it if you don't."

"Thanks, Coach Brown," I said.

I knew keeping the dog away from school might be a problem, but I didn't say so. I wanted to get the dog home.

➤

Chapter

20

Coach Brown led the way, while we walked through the woods, searching for the dog. As I turned to leave the wooded area, the dog appeared. The retriever brought a small twig to play a game of fetch. We threw the twig two times for the dog to chase. Once the retriever returned the twig a second time, I hooked a leash on the dog. I led it to the front of the school. Coach Brown helped me place the dog in Mom's car. I thanked him and waved good-bye. During the ride with Mom, I was eager to tell her about the school day.

"The golden retriever stayed by my side during reading.

The dog looked like it was reading from my book."

"I guess you liked having the dog next to you, didn't you? You didn't get into trouble because of it, did you?"

"No. I liked having it there, but I didn't touch the dog."

When Mom and I were home, I put the dog in the backyard. I needed to make phone calls, so I hurried though my homework and chores. I wanted to be sure that I had enough time for archery and baseball. As I started to leave for the school practices, the phone rang. I recognized Jake's voice when I answered it.

"Are you ready for archery practice?"

"I'm coming now," I said.

Jake and I didn't talk anymore. We wanted to get in lots of practice time.

On the way to Jake's, I pretended I was an Olympic runner: a sprinter. I ran until a bark caused me to stop. I decided the bark came from a neighbor's house. It didn't seem like the bark of the golden retriever, because my house was so far away. When I spun around, I saw the dog racing toward me. I liked having the dog, but I didn't want to be late getting to my friend's house. Somehow the dog had escaped. It must have dug its way out.

I started back home with the dog at my heels. When I arrived, I put the dog in the backyard. I secured the gate and petted the dog. To keep the dog in the backyard, I put a couple of boards under one high area of the fence. That area seemed to have a gap between the ground and the fence where the dog had escaped.

I phoned Jake to be sure he didn't leave me. Jake laughed when he heard my story of why I was late. I promised him I'd hurry to make up for the lost time. In a matter of minutes, I arrived at Jake's. He was waiting for me.

"That dog thinks you're part of its pack," Jake said.

"My parents let me keep the dog this week. I will have to find an owner for it."

"That dog belongs to you, Matt. Haven't you convinced your parents yet?"

"I want the dog, but my parents don't."

"You've got to beg them. Volunteer to do extra jobs around the house. Maybe they'll let you keep the dog then."

"Dad said, 'No.' I asked to adopt the dog several times, but he made me drop the subject. I don't want to be grounded."

"You have to talk at the right time. You've got to come up with a plan to keep the dog. Your parents could change their minds."

"My parents plan to adopt a dog after the family vacation. I want the grown retriever, though. Do you think your parents would keep the dog for a while? I could try changing my parents' minds," I said.

"I doubt that my parents will keep it, but I'll try. Do you want to wait while I ask them?" Jake asked.

"Isn't your dad at work?"

"No. He took a vacation day. I'll ask them now. Wait here."

"I'll stand outside," I said.

While Jake talked to his parents, I viewed the large oak and pine trees in the neighborhood. I stood, admiring the trees until a boy rode his bicycle past me. He pedaled ahead before fading into the background. But in a few minutes, brakes squealed. A crowd gathered at the crosswalk down the street.

When I pushed into the crowd, I recognized the boy hit. He was the one who'd just gone by me. I ran to Jake's house to get help for him. Once I was a few feet from Jake's front door, I yelled.

"Jake, I need to call 911! A boy has been hit by a car."

Jake appeared and handed me the phone. I punched in the emergency number.

When the dispatcher answered, I gave details about the accident to him. While I talked, Jake's parents grabbed towels for the victim. After I got off the phone, Jake's family and I ran to the accident site. Jake's mother used the towels to put pressure on the boy's wounds, as she sat beside him.

Within minutes, the paramedics had the boy in an ambulance. When Jake and I turned to go to archery practice, a policeman thanked us for helping the boy.

"Is the boy all right, officer?" I asked.

"Your quick thinking helped the boy," the policeman said.

I felt better after hearing the policeman's words. I wanted the boy to live. By the time Jake and I arrived at practice, my thoughts were on archery, not the accident.

Jake, Ben, and I shot arrows for over an hour. The practice sessions for the last few weeks had paid off. I hit the target three times; my other arrows landed close to the center.

My friends didn't do as well in the beginning, but before long they hit the bull's-eye. All of us were improving a little each day.

During baseball practice, Jake and I hit several home runs. But then, I didn't make it to one base before the second baseman put me out. Even though I didn't smile the rest of the game, I didn't complain. Making the out was my fault.

Jake and I chatted nonstop on the way home. I didn't want to run, like we did sometimes, because I'd just run in baseball. We walked slowly to begin with, but then we sped up. I had chores to finish before bedtime. Right before Jake and I split up, he told me that his parents would keep the dog over my family's vacation. Now, I planned to talk to my parents again about the dog adoption.

At home, Mom had a new dish baking in the oven. I worked on my chores before dinner. That day, I decided not to put off anything anymore.

I completed my chores before dinner. They didn't take too long, so I concentrated on what I'd say to my parents about keeping the dog.

While my family ate together, I said little. I waited for the right moment to bring up the dog adoption. I hoped I could change their minds about the dog. *Perhaps if they knew Jake would keep the dog during my vacation, they would agree to let me keep the dog.*

I watched Dad sit in his favorite chair. He was staring at the television blankly, so I knew he wasn't working on anything important. I decided now was the best time to bring up the dog adoption.

"Dad," I said, but then I paused.

"What do you want?" Dad asked.

"Jake says that he'll take care of the dog during our vacation. Would you let me keep the dog after that?"

"I thought I'd told you not to bring that subject up again."

"I know, Dad, but . . . "

Dad interrupted, "Why are you so intent on having that dog?"

"I like it. The dog's friendly; besides, it thinks I'm its master."

"That's because you've fed and petted it, Matt."

"It's not just that. The dog follows me everywhere. At school, the dog even sits beside me in the reading group."

"I will discuss the dog with you later. Right now, I just want to relax."

Dad didn't give me the answer I wanted to hear. He hadn't really given me an answer at all. I needed for him to change his mind about the dog.

➤

Chapter

21

I went to my bedroom, waiting for Dad. When he entered my
room, I felt ready to discuss the dog adoption. The time I'd spent
alone had helped me think of the right words to say to Dad. I'd
practiced the words, so I cleared my throat.

"Dad, I want to keep the grown dog. I've taught it to obey
commands. I'm willing to do extra chores to keep it. Will you let
me have the dog?" I said.

"You've got a point. I don't like leaving the dog in
another person's care, while we're gone, though. What if it flees
and hurts someone?"

"The dog's never hurt any of us."

"That's true, but that doesn't mean it won't," Dad said.

"Jake's spent time with the dog. I'm sure he'll take good care of it."

"Call Jake now. I want to talk to him and his parents," Dad said.

I rushed to the phone. I didn't want to wait another minute to adopt the dog. Once I punched in Jake's number, his phone kept ringing. His mother answered right before I hung up.

"Hello, Mrs. Graham. Is Jake home?" I asked.

"He's here. I'll get him."

I waited for Jake, while pumping my feet back and forth. During our conversation, I told Jake about Dad's concerns. I smiled when Jake agreed to talk with Dad.

I stood as close to the phone as possible. I listened to Dad ask Jake and his mom several questions. Dad's conversation didn't last long, but I was unable to hear what Jake's family said.

Once Dad put the phone away, his face didn't indicate whether we'd keep the dog or not. When he smiled and spoke, I felt better.

"If our family adopts the dog, are you willing to assume responsibility for it?" Dad asked.

"You mean — like feeding the dog?"

"That's just one thing you'd need to do, Matt. The dog will need bath time and playtime."

I nodded to indicate *yes.* "I can handle all that. I'll have a playmate," I said.

"Dogs dig, so you might have to fill in holes with dirt."

"It's an adult dog, so it probably won't dig as much," I said.

Dad chuckled. "All dogs dig. They like to hide bones to eat later. If they're left alone for long periods, they can get into mischief."

"I'll play with the dog, so it won't get into trouble. The rest of our family can help pet and play with it, too."

"I guess we can try the dog. Do you have a backup plan, if things don't work out?"

"Everything will be fine. Thank you, Dad," I replied while jumping up and down.

"If the dog becomes a problem, we'll have to get rid of

it," Dad said.

"Did you tell Jake we plan to adopt the dog?" I asked.

"When Jake questioned me about the dog, I told him we're adopting it. Jake will pick up the dog tomorrow, so the dog can adjust to being around a different place. It's hard to believe no one ever claimed the dog, since so many people tried to find the owner. The dog had no chip implanted in it for locating its owner. "

"Oh, but I like having the retriever here. We don't leave for two days," I said.

"You'll have plenty of time with the dog after our trip," Dad replied. "That dog needs time to get readjusted to Jake."

"I wish we could take it on the trip."

"Don't even consider that. We're not bringing the dog with us. Some hotels require you to pay more when you bring a dog with you. We can't take the dog with us every time we go to a new place. Restaurants don't allow dogs. Hotel rooms can be lonely places for pets."

"Why do hotels make you pay more for having a dog?"

"Dogs get things dirty; they tear up things."

"I wouldn't let the dog do that. Couldn't we take it, please?" I begged.

"No. There will be no dog at all, if you keep begging to take it on the trip. While we sightsee, a dog doesn't need to be alone. The car gets too hot to leave it in."

"I wish we could leave on the vacation now. I can't wait until the dog is my own."

"Had you rather stay with the retriever than go on a vacation?" Dad questioned.

"No, I guess not," I said. "I will miss the dog, though."

"I know you will enjoy the trip. Get your pajamas on. It's almost bedtime."

Chapter

22

Today was the last school day for the year. Ms. Winthrop had planned fun activities: a play, some games, a story, and a party. Classmates were to share their summer plans. I looked forward to the party most of all. The party favors, games, and refreshments made the day special.

Sharing time began in the morning. It was a lot more fun than the morning written work. I looked forward to sharing my good news when the teacher called on me.

"My family will get a new member. Can you guess when it will arrive?"

"No," Lynn said. "Is it a baby?"

"Oh, Matt's going to be a brother, I guess," said Ben.

The class started talking and laughing; the noise level increased. My teacher settled everyone down for me to finish talking.

"No. My mother's not having a baby," I said. "I'm getting a new dog soon. That's a special surprise for me. For my family's vacation, we plan to go to a Florida beach. I can't wait to swim in the ocean, go to a museum, and visit a zoo. Of course, eating out will be great. There will be no dishes to load in the dishwasher."

I grinned when Jake volunteered to be next. He told how he planned to care for my dog during my vacation. Jake also mentioned his family's plans to go to Germany. By the time he'd finished speaking, I wanted to go there, too.

Once sharing time ended, all the teachers put on a play for the classes. The costumes, actions, and songs kept me watching every minute. Each time something funny happened, Jake and I laughed together. Hearing his belly laugh caused me to laugh loudly. When I'd been sad about not having the dog, he'd helped cheer me up with his jokes and laughter. Today, we were both just having fun. After the play was over, my class had lunch and story time. Finally, it was time for physical education, so the teacher lined us up. I rushed to be the first in line.

Like the play I'd watched earlier, physical education ended before I wanted it to. I almost got into trouble lining up, by talking too much. I had to be careful, because I didn't want to miss any fun activities. The math and spelling bees took more concentration than other activities, but they were fun. I looked forward to finding out what I'd learned for the year.

Around one o'clock, my class played games. Some of us got a little too noisy then. I was quiet during the snack preparation time, since Mom was there. I knew I'd get into trouble, if I didn't behave. As the noise level increased again, the teacher held up her red warning sign. I knew she meant business. I wanted my class to settle down, because I didn't want to lose the party time. The class might have more written work, too. I didn't want that.

While the snacks were served, my classmates kept their voices down. When the last bell rang, everyone raced out.

My friends and I hurried to get home. I was anxious for the summer activities to begin, and I wanted to see my dog. The walk didn't take long, so that left an hour to spend with the dog. Dad and I planned to take the retriever over to Jake's later. I ran through the kitchen once I was home, but I didn't stop.

I called out, "Mom, I'm home."

I smiled when I glanced at Mom talking on the phone. The call would keep her busy for a while. I would have more time to give my dog attention, so I rushed outside.

The time flew by as I played with the retriever. I threw its toy squirrel, and I praised the dog when it returned the squirrel. Once I went inside, I studied a list of names to give the dog. I had decided on the name Allie when Mom called me.

"Matt, it's time to take the dog to Jake's house. Your father is here to help you."

Before Dad was ready to leave, I took the dog's food and bowls to the car. I led my dog, Allie, outside after attaching the leash to its collar. Once Dad, Allie, and I arrived at Jake's, I helped Jake get Allie into his backyard. I didn't linger saying good-bye to Jake or Allie, because Dad had told me to hurry. It was hard to leave Allie behind, though.

"I'll take good care of your dog. You have fun," Jake said.

"I'll try, but I'll miss my dog," I said.

On the way home, Dad asked why I was quiet. I had trouble answering his question, because I didn't like leaving Allie. I knew my family's trip would be short, but it was hard telling Allie good-bye for a few days. Dad drove to our house without stopping, since it was time for dinner.

At the end of the dinner conversation, Mom gave me instructions for the next day. She handed me a suitcase, and she told me to pack my clothes for the trip. As soon as I had the case in my hands, I packed several pairs of shorts, shirts, socks, and underwear. My swim trunks and a towel went into the suitcase, too. The last thing I packed was my bag of toys, games, and books. Before I turned in for the night, I had something important to do. I punched in Jake's number to be sure Allie was happy and safe.

"Hello," Jake answered in a raspy voice. "Who's calling?"

"This is Matt. Did I wake you up?" I asked.

"Yes. Why are you calling so late?"

"I was checking on Allie," I said.

"Who's Allie?" Jake asked, like he was half asleep.

"You know — the dog."

"Oh, Allie's fine. Why didn't you say the dog?"

"I thought you knew I meant the dog. I'm glad Allie's fine. I'm sorry I woke you. Good-bye."

I put my phone away, since Jake said nothing else. He'd started snoring. I read until my book fell to the floor. I put it away, and I slept.

The next morning, I ate breakfast, dressed, and cleaned my room. I asked for permission to see my dog at Jake's. Once I had Dad's permission to leave, I headed to Jake's, whistling the whole way. As I walked closer to his house, a familiar bark caused me to hurry ahead. The bark had to be Allie's, because Jake had no dog.

I rang the doorbell at Jake's. After his mother answered the door, she invited me to his room. Jake appeared to be sleeping when I entered his room. As soon as I stood next to him,

I heard a loud noise.

"Boo!" Jake yelled.

Jake's voice made me jump while he laughed. I waited for him to get dressed. We planned to play with Allie together. Even though Jake hurried, he wasn't fast enough for me.

I had hoped we could slip up on Allie. That was impossible to do. When we got to the fence, the dog sat, waiting. It wagged its tail to welcome us. I put the dog's leash on its collar. Jake and I walked Allie around the block, since I had an hour to spend at Jake's.

By the time we finished walking Allie, it was time for me to leave Jake's house. I rushed home, but I didn't like leaving Allie.

That evening, the television time was short. My family planned to leave early the next day. We had a long drive, and Dad wanted to check into a hotel before dark. I helped Dad pack the car. Loading the car took a lot of energy, so I didn't have to be told to sleep afterwards. I went right to bed.

The next day, I read books and played games as Dad drove to Florida. Dad didn't take many breaks, but he stopped when we needed to stretch our legs. I looked forward to the breaks. During one break, my family got to choose one snack they wanted to eat. Dad bought something for each person.

We drove for a long spell without stopping. When it was getting dark, I called Jake. I wanted to see how Allie was doing. I laughed when Jake shared some of the dog stories. At the end of our conversation, I was concerned about two things: *What if Allie got lost? What if Dad asked why I was laughing?*

I didn't tell Dad right away what Allie had been doing. Even though I heard Dad's question clearly, I tried to avoid answering it.

"Why were you laughing?" Dad asked.

"Oh, Allie did something funny."

"Well, tell us, so we can laugh," Dad said.

My mind raced, thinking of what to say. I stalled, but I had to answer Dad. My words didn't seem like a good explanation, but Dad kept pushing me for an answer. I took a deep breath before I said a word, and it gave me the courage to tell him everything.

By the time I'd finished speaking, I'd told Dad how the

dog had slipped away. Dad had warned me that the dog might get loose. I didn't want Dad to be upset with me.

"I hope Allie stays away from dangerous places. How did the dog get out this time?" Dad asked.

"I'm not sure. Allie used to wander into our classroom when we were reading. I guess the retriever wanted attention," I said to him. "Maybe Jake didn't have the fence secured properly."

"Having the dog on the loose could create some problems for us," Dad said.

"Like what?" I asked.

"Allie could bite someone. Or the dogcatcher could get the dog. I hope Jake can secure Allie in his backyard."

I hadn't even considered the dogcatcher, so I called Jake again. I felt better after Jake assured me that the dog was back in his backyard. Jake's father had helped him secure the dog's area. I told my parents what Jake had said.

➤

Chapter

23

While Dad checked us into the hotel, I begged to visit the ocean.
Even though Mom started walking with me, I darted ahead. I
removed my shoes, leaving them on the shore. I loved playing in
the foamy waves, and I enjoyed watching the fading sunlight.
The waves pulled strongly against my feet in the shallow waters.
I wanted to go farther into the ocean. Before I walked very far,
Mom called.

"Matt, come back. You need an adult with you when you
swim."

I wanted to stay where I was, but I stopped. Floating on

my raft would be so much fun now. I had to obey Mom, because I wanted to be able to swim later.

Once I moved close to Mom, I asked for permission to play in the shallow part. While I played there, the sea plants floated around me. I played in the waves until a small fish bumped into me. I bolted away from it at first, but then I realized it was harmless. As I started to follow it, Mom called me again.

"Your dad needs help unloading the car. We can come back after we get things put away. Come along now."

Mom walked ahead of me. I tried to catch up with her, but moving through the sand slowed me down. The moist sand felt like a cushion below my feet. Leaving my footprints in the sand was fun. When Mom and I reached the car, I grabbed for Mom's suitcase. It felt like it had a pile of bricks in it, so Dad had to lift it.

My family's hotel room had two stuffed chairs, two beds, and a television in it. The room also had a refrigerator, chest, closet, and a desk. Without wasting a minute, I unpacked my things. I was ready to swim at the beach. While Mom unpacked, I used the restroom to change into my swim trunks. Afterwards, I read until the whole family had unpacked and changed clothes. When my family was ready, we walked to the beach.

At the beach, I floated and played on my raft until a wave knocked me off. When I regained my balance, I stood a few feet from a boy I didn't know. He looked to be about my age, so we talked and played with each other. The boy told me his name was Tim. We rode the waves together for a while. Later, Tim and I played with a beach ball.

Once Tim and I left the water, we played a game of volleyball with his friends. Every time my team scored, my parents cheered. At the end of the game, my family returned to the hotel room to change from our wet swimsuits.

Early in the afternoon, my family and I ate lunch. We drove down the beach shop area after eating. Dad drove us in both directions along the beach. Our family enjoyed shopping at several shops on the main highway. I was having so much fun that I almost forgot to call Jake.

As Dad drove toward our hotel, I called Jake. I couldn't get him at first, so I decided to call Ben. I longed to know how Allie was doing. I knew Ben would check on the dog for me.

Dad drove several miles during my conversation with Ben. The details Ben told about Allie's escape caused me to shake. I didn't stay upset long after I realized how funny Allie was. I said little during the conversation with Ben, because I wanted to know about the dog's escapades. I placed the phone close to my ear, because I didn't want to miss any part of the details.

"Allie escaped by digging under the fence again. Anyway, Jake and I hunted for the dog everywhere. We didn't see Allie for thirty minutes. When we walked by the library, I suggested going inside," Ben said.

"Why did you go in there?"

"We wanted to put contact information on the bulletin board inside the library. We planned to put up a sign about Allie being lost. Before we put the information on the board, we received a surprise."

I was anxious to hear the rest of the story, but Ben needed to clear his throat. He sounded hoarse. I was in a hurry.

"So, go on," I said.

"The children's librarian had a large group in her room,"

Ben continued. "We couldn't see what was going on until Jake and I got farther inside. Right beside the librarian was Allie," Ben said, giggling.

"You're kidding, right?" I asked.

"No, I'm not. And Allie had her eyes fixed on the librarian. The dog looked like a reading dog. Having Allie there caused the kids to become more fascinated with the library. After a few minutes, the librarian entertained the children with a book. She promised everyone a visit with Allie once the book was read. At the end of the reading period, the photographer snapped pictures."

"Why did the photographer take pictures?"

"I think they want the pictures to promote the summer reading program," Ben said.

"I like that idea. Did the dog create any problems?"

"None that I know of. In fact, more kids kept coming in to sign up for the reading program. They wanted to see the dog. Two hundred or more kids signed up for the summer program."

"Did the librarian like having the dog there?"

"I'm sure she did. The librarian smiled the whole time, as

kids kept coming in."

"Were you and Jake able to get Allie back into Jake's yard?"

"We used the magic word *treat* to get her inside. Allie waited patiently for the bones we had. As soon as the dog went inside the fence, we placed boards under another spot where the fence didn't touch the ground. We made sure the gate latch was pushed down, too," Ben stated.

"Call me, if there is a problem with Allie. You have my cell number, don't you?"

"Yes. I'll call, if there's a problem. We're having fun with the dog."

Once I put the phone away, I was sorry that I'd missed Allie putting on a show at the library. I hoped the dog would get another invitation to the library when I returned home. Allie might just turn up there again. I didn't want the retriever to get me into trouble, though.

After my conversation with Ben, I told Mom and Dad about Allie's adventures. While Mom and I laughed together, Dad didn't laugh; he had a solemn look on his face. I wondered what Dad was thinking once I shared Allie's adventures with the family.

"I thought you told me the dog was secured better this time," Dad said.

"Allie must have dug its way out of a another spot."

"That's a problem. We should have waited to get a dog," Dad said.

"I think Allie will be fine. Jake and Ben have placed boards under the fence, so it can't get out. The dog's library visit brought more kids into the summer reading program. Ben told me how photographers took Allie's picture with the librarian and the kids."

➤

Chapter

24

I looked for my new beach friend the next morning, but Tim
wasn't at our meeting place. Once Dad entered the water, I asked
to go out deeper. I grabbed my raft, joining Dad when he
signaled me to follow. I rode the waves for an hour, but I
frowned when Dad stopped me. My frown changed after he
announced our next surprise: a space center visit.

The spaceships, suits, and launch pictures gave me the
idea of becoming an astronaut. I wanted to do experiments in a
different environment outside the spaceship. Venus would be
interesting to visit. I knew it would be too hot to survive there,

though.

In the late afternoon, my family dined at a restaurant that jutted out over the ocean. I watched the small fish swim in a school, not far away. There were few large fish swimming close to where the restaurant was. When the waiter brought my crab meal, I struggled to use my cracking tool. Mom showed me how to use it. By using Mom's suggestion, I scooped out every bite from the crab claws.

I walked with Dad back to the hotel along the shoreline. Mom took the car back. As the sun sank lower in the sky, I waded in the water. I liked the feel of the gentle waves on my feet. While we walked, I searched for shells. I checked for a living creature inside of each one; I didn't want to disturb any living animal. During my search, I studied the shell markings and sizes. I walked several yards along the beach, trying to find other shells. Most of them were broken, but I kept looking for whole ones.

The cool breeze and the crashing waves made me want to sleep outdoors; I knew my parents wouldn't allow that. Before I walked far, Dad called. I wasn't ready to go, so I lingered on the shore. By the time I tried to catch Dad, he was almost out of sight.

"Wait, Dad," I called.

"Hurry. We might get an ice cream before the parlor closes."

My dad didn't have to call another time. I wanted an ice cream. In a short time, we stood in an ice cream parlor. When I heard someone call my name, I turned around. To my surprise, Tim and his family were there.

When Tim motioned for me to come over, I told Dad which ice cream flavor I wanted. I rushed to Tim's bench.

"Get your ice cream and sit here," Tim said.

"I'll be there in a minute. Will you be here for a while?"

"We'll be here, since my parents just bought their ice cream. They're talking to some friends," Tim said.

I went to the counter where Dad handed me my pistachio cone. I liked it because of the taste, color, and nuts. Once Dad gave his approval to sitting with Tim, I headed to his bench. I licked the cone sides to keep it from dripping.

"Where were you today? I didn't see you?" I questioned

Tim.

"My mom made me do chores before tennis practice. By the time I'd finished everything, there wasn't time for playing on the beach. Let's meet in front of your hotel tomorrow," Tim remarked.

"We usually go to the beach from nine to eleven in the morning. Will you be there then?" I asked.

"I'll try."

Tim and I made our plans while we ate the cones. When Mom called, I had to leave. My parents wanted us in bed before ten.

As we dressed for bed, Dad announced sightseeing plans for tomorrow. I didn't know how to contact Tim, since I didn't have his phone number. I paused before speaking to Dad, trying to think of what to say.

"Dad, I thought we planned to swim tomorrow morning. Couldn't we go for a little while?"

"We won't have time to go to the beach tomorrow morning. Our sightseeing trip is too far away."

"I didn't know the family had plans already. I promised

Tim I'd meet him at the beach in the morning," I said.

"Call him to let him know you won't be there."

"I don't have his number and last name, so I can't call him."

"We'll try to get an early start. That way, we'll have time to stop and tell him why you can't play tomorrow. What time were you planning to meet him?"

"Around nine or ten."

"I'll drive to the parking area close to where you're to meet Tim. You can walk down the steps to tell him you can't play," Dad said.

I thought about Dad's suggestion. I couldn't do anything else without Tim's phone number.

Early the next morning, I dressed quickly. I wanted to meet my friend before sightseeing. I read a book while my parents dressed. We walked out the door at eight o'clock.

I took my backpack full of games and books for entertainment in the car. The sightseeing place was a distance down the road, so I knew I'd have plenty of time to read and play. I really wanted to play with Tim, but my parents had other plans.

Once breakfast ended, I reminded Dad that I needed to talk to Tim. Dad walked with me to the spot Tim and I had agreed upon, and Mom waited in the car. We stood in the area for over five minutes, but there was no sign of Tim. I quickly scrawled a note to leave him on the handrail.

Dear Tim,

I'm sorry I missed you. Dad had made family plans I didn't know about for this morning. I can't play today, but I can play on the beach tomorrow. If you can't make it tomorrow, please leave me a note here.

Your friend,

Matt

I taped the note to the handrail, leading from the hotel to the beach. I hoped Tim would see the note.

When I returned to the car, Mom mentioned my serious expression. I didn't feel like explaining my friend's absence, but I told Mom what had happened. While Dad drove from the beach, I pulled out two games and a book. I planned to read and play during our drive.

For the first part of the sightseeing trip, Dad drove us to an amusement park. I passed through the turnstile, hurrying to the first ride ahead. I wanted to go on each ride several times.

"Which ride do you want to go on first?" Dad asked.

"The roller coaster. Mom, are you going with us?" I asked.

"I'll go on some rides, but not that one. Are you sure you want to ride on one that high and fast?"

"Oh, I can't wait to ride it."

"I'll wait for both of you by the ticket counter," Mom said.

I hurried to a seat up front. During the ride, my stomach turned flips. I took delight in having the wind blow my face and hair. It was a real adventure to be up so high. Dad and I joined Mom at the end of the roller coaster ride. Once Mom stared at my windblown hair, she handed me a comb. I thought combing my hair was a waste of time. I raked the comb through my hair anyway.

Before I rode anything else, my family walked around the

amusement park. On our walk, we spotted a tiny dog and a young girl. I didn't like the idea of being close to a girl, but I wanted to pet the dog. Mom and Dad walked over toward the dog and girl, so I joined them.

Once I gave the girl a compliment on her dog, she stopped; she let me pet her dog. I scratched behind the dog's ears, and my parents talked to the girl named Emily for a while. She told us her dog's name was Sunshine. I was anxious to go on the rides, so we parted.

By the time I'd finished going on every ride once, I was starving. I began looking for food vendors.

"Are we eating soon?" I asked.

"I think we're all hungry. We can stop at the hot dog stand," Dad said.

"Is there a place to sit at the stand? It looks crowded," Mom commented.

"Someone might leave by the time we get our food," Dad said.

"I can stand, if there aren't enough seats. I see at least two seats," I said.

"We'll find a seat for everyone," Dad remarked.

My family found three seats after we received our food. The table wasn't far from Emily and Sunshine. While we ate, the dog entertained us with its actions. The dog's moves made me think of Allie. I missed sharing Allie's adventures with Jake and Ben. I decided to call Jake to find out how Allie was doing, but no one answered his phone.

"Who did you call?" Dad asked.

"Jake. No one answered. I needed to check on Allie."

"He might be walking Allie," Mom said.

"I'll try him later."

Even though I hadn't reached Jake, I sat admiring Allie's photograph at the amusement park. I decided my dog was snuggling up to someone it liked. At that moment, I missed Allie terribly.

As our family walked along, I tried Jake's number again. His phone rang and rang, but there was no answer. Several questions came into my mind while we walked. *What if Allie wanted to be at the library all the time? What if the dogcatcher caught Allie?* I put those thoughts out of my mind, as I climbed into the car.

For the family's next adventure, we went to a small zoo. I watched the alligator show from a fence. The alligators were interesting to watch from a distance, but we were not allowed to be too close to them. While we were at the zoo, we saw huge turtles, monkeys, and birds. I could have stayed there all day, watching the animals. After two hours, we left. My parents didn't like being in the hot temperature outside. Once we returned to the car, Dad stopped at a store to purchase a snow cone or soft drink for everyone. Of course, I chose a cherry snow cone.

During the drive to the hotel, I read a book for thirty minutes. Once I put my book away, I jotted down things I'd learned on the trip. Writing down details gave me an idea. *We could have a story contest at the library? An animal could be a character in the stories.* Before long, I had listed several ideas for the story contest. I wanted to share my ideas with the librarian when I returned home.

➤

Chapter

25

I looked forward to a beach stroll that evening, but Dad wanted

to skip the evening walk. The sounds of the band playing outside

caused Dad to change his mind. Dad sat in a lounge chair, and

Mom and I ambled along the beach.

During our walk, a distant marina captured my attention.

I wanted to take a boat ride right then. Disappointment set in

when I found out it was too late to go on a fishing boat.

As the sky darkened, I used a small flashlight to find

small sea animals and shells around. When it was time to go in, I

heard a familiar voice in the distance. I didn't know which

direction the voice came from. I saw Tim's family about the time Dad joined Mom and me. I signaled for Tim to stop.

"Hey, Tim. Wait for me," I said. "Did you find the note I left you today?"

"No. Where did you leave it?"

"I taped it to the handrail over there," I said.

"Maybe it blew away," Tim suggested. "I didn't find a note there."

"I couldn't meet you today. Dad had plans to take us sightseeing. He had not told me before we talked. I didn't have your phone number to call you, so I left you a note. Will you meet me around nine o'clock tomorrow?" I asked.

"Yes, I think I can meet you. Let's give each other our phone numbers. That way, if something unexpected happens, we can let each other know."

I had no paper, but Mom usually carried some in her purse. When I asked her for a sheet, Mom pulled out a bent pad of paper. I tore off the first wrinkled sheet, wadding it up. I split the next sheet into two parts. On one part, I wrote my whole name and phone number. I gave Tim that piece. On the second part, I wrote Tim's name and number. I kept that piece for myself. That way, we had contact information on each other.

Later in the evening, I fell asleep watching television. I slept until the sunlight awakened me. I stood up, and I stretched without making a sound. I did not want to awaken my parents.

I crept to the window. People were already on the beach. I stood there for ten minutes, and my parents slept. I grabbed my clothes, washed, and dressed. When I returned to the room, Mom lifted her head.

"Why are you up so early?" she whispered.

"I have to meet Tim in thirty minutes. We haven't eaten breakfast."

"We'll make it. I'll wake Dad. We can grab something at the eatery downstairs."

At the breakfast area, Dad ordered each of us a ham biscuit. I ate fast; I wanted to be on time to meet Tim. When we returned to our hotel room, I threw on my swim trunks.

I frowned when Mom brought up her rule: no swimming for an hour after eating. I'd eaten twenty minutes ago. Once I joined Tim, I shared Mom's swimming rule with him. We piled up sand, making a sand castle and a fort. I hoped our sand sculptures were far enough from the waves, so they wouldn't be destroyed.

An hour after eating, Tim and I rode the waves with our rafts. We used our hands for paddling to the shoreline. When Mom called me to lunch, I didn't want to stop.

"Good-bye, Tim," I said. "Maybe we can play later."

"Will you be able to play a game of table tennis this afternoon? We could meet at the recreation center at two o'clock," Tim suggested.

"I think so, but let me check with my parents. Where is the recreation center?"

"It's only four blocks away on Palm Street. Turn right to get on Main Beach Parkway. Make a left turn at Palm Street, which is about three blocks down. The recreation center will be at 102 Palm Street. It will be on your right side. I'll wait here while you ask your Mom about going."

"I'll be right back," I said.

I looked for Mom. I found her under an umbrella in her rose swimsuit. It took time to find her, because there were so many people on the beach. I ran to her when I found her sitting in a lawn chair. I was out of breath, so I gasped for air.

"Mom, could I meet Tim at the recreation center at two o'clock today? We want to play table tennis," I said.

"Where is the recreation center?"

I answered Mom's question. She agreed for me to play on one condition: I had to call Jake and check on my dog first. I had no problem with her condition, so I ran back to where Tim stood.

"I'll meet you later to play table tennis," I said.

Once my family reached our hotel room, we took showers and dressed. Before the noon meal, I grabbed my backpack. I read a book as we drove to the restaurant. When I called Jake, he answered his phone on the second ring.

"Hello, Jake. How is Allie?"

"Man, do I have big news for you," Jake began.

"Tell me quickly. Dad is driving us to eat lunch. We'll be at the restaurant soon."

"I walked to the library this morning. Guess who was there?"

"Who?"

"Ms. Winthrop stood by the front desk, checking out several books. She asked me about Allie."

"I told her how Allie likes the library. Ms. Winthrop wants you to bring Allie to her class when school starts again. She wants you to give a demonstration of the dog reading beside you."

"If you see Ms. Winthrop again, tell her I'll bring Allie to school. I think Mom can help me with the dog. Of course, I'll have to check Mom's calendar to be sure she's free that day."

"I wish we were in our old room again. It was fun to have the dog in our class," Jake said.

"The retriever made me laugh a lot," I said.

"Me, too."

"Well, Dad wants me to eat now. I'll try calling tomorrow," I said.

"Do you know when you will be home?" Jake asked.

"I think I'll be home in two or three days. I can tell you tomorrow."

Jake and I ended our conversation, because my family wanted to eat. We hurried to finish our meal, since it was almost time to meet Tim.

Once Tim and I began our table tennis game, I knew I was no match for him. Every time I hit the ball over the net, Tim hit it directly in my court. I wasn't able to return it fast enough. I had trouble making a single point.

"How many days a week do you practice?" I asked Tim.

Tim laughed. "Well, I don't practice every day, but I play five or six times a week."

"Mom says practice helps."

"Some of my friends play better than I do. They practice more often. Conner practices every day," Tim replied.

"I have no chance of winning if he's better than you."

"Would you like to play doubles? I could ask Conner and John to play with us."

"No. Let me learn how to play first. Maybe we could play with them later."

"Suit yourself. Table tennis is more fun when you play with a teammate. You might do better with a friend than by yourself."

"You think so?"

"Yes. Do you want to try playing with a teammate?"

"I'll try playing doubles," I said.

I stood anxiously at the table beside Tim, because the game was so new to me. When Conner and John took their positions, I hit the ball over the net. I had trouble returning the ball when Conner slammed it into my court. My face turned red, like a clown's face decorated with paint.

I played better as the game continued. I was no match for the other players, though. When Mom drove up, I had to ask for a time out to talk to her.

"We need to finish the game," I pleaded with Mom. "Will you give me a few more minutes? The game is tied."

"Can you wrap up the game in fifteen minutes?"

"I think so," I said.

"You have only fifteen minutes," Mom told me.

When Conner slammed the ball into my court, I wasn't able to return it again. I knew I'd lost the game for my team. My face felt on fire. Even though I was upset, Tim didn't seem to be. I told him that I was sorry.

"The game is fun. I like for my team to win; we can't win

every time, though. We might win next time," Tim stated.

"With a new teammate, you might win," I suggested.

"You aren't giving up that easily, are you?" Tim asked.

"No, but someone who's played more might do better. Today was the first time I've played this game."

"I liked having you on my team. You'll become a pro with practice," Tim said.

"Thanks for letting me play with you. I have to run now. Mom is motioning for me to come. Will you call later?"

"Yes," Tim answered. "Maybe we can play again before you have to go to your home."

"Are you sure that you still want me on your team?"

"Yes. I like playing doubles. You'll improve. It's fun to play with friends."

"We'll see. I'll talk to you later. Thanks for inviting me," I said.

➤

Chapter

26

I tried all sorts of ways to get Dad to reveal a surprise he'd promised me. Without any clues, I had to wait until Dad wanted to tell me. I was hoping he'd tell me at dinnertime. Earlier, I'd asked Mom about the surprise. She was in on the secret, so it didn't help to ask her about it. While I waited to find out what the surprise was, I played a game from my backpack. Concentrating on the game was impossible: I was trying to figure out what the surprise was.

When I asked questions again, Dad told me to hush. For an hour and a half, I read. My family left for dinner at half past five. I still didn't know what the surprise was.

The meal lasted a long time because of all the courses. I didn't mention the surprise during the meal. After eating dessert, I thought Dad would share the surprise with me. He said nothing until the waitress left.

"It's almost time for the surprise," Dad said.

I wanted the surprise now, but I tried to be patient. Waiting for the surprise was hard. Dad had not told me what the surprise was yet.

"Have you guessed what your surprise is?"

"No," I said. "What is it?"

"I guess I've made you wait long enough. Tim's family and our family are going to play miniature golf tonight. We have to hurry to meet them by half past seven. Do you like that surprise?"

"You bet. Will Tim and I be able to meet at the beach in the morning?"

"Tomorrow you may, but after that you may not. We'll be going home. You'll be able to see your dog again."

"Oh, I have to call Jake when we start home. He needs to

know what time we'll arrive."

"You may call him now if you'd like."

I called Jake, but no one answered at first. When I started to hang up, Jake answered.

"Hi, Matt, what's up?"

"How did you know it was me?"

"I saw your number come up on the phone screen," Jake said.

"I called to let you know which day we're coming home."

"I hope it's not today, because I'm having fun with your dog. The librarian asked me to bring it to the library tomorrow. She wants Allie for the children's story time."

"You may take Allie. I can't go. We're leaving two days from now. It might be late when we arrive, so I'll probably get Allie the next morning. I'll call when we get close. Will you be home that evening?"

"I think so. You can always leave a message," Jake said.

"We'll get together. It will be fun to participate in other reading activities with Allie. Are other library events planned?"

"Yes. All the summer reading kids like Allie. You'll be back in time for the dog's other library appearance," Jake said.

"When will the next event be?"

"The date will be August 5th."

"I'll tell Mom, so she can put it on the calendar. Do you have the date for the school reading event?"

"Ms. Winthrop's event is for the second day of school. I don't have a calendar to give you the date right now."

"I will get that date later. I have to go now and meet Tim's family. They are waiting to play miniature golf."

"Who's Tim?" Jake asked.

"He's a friend I met at the beach. I've got to go now, but I'll call you tomorrow."

"Have fun. I'll talk to you later," Jake said.

When my family arrived at the miniature golf course, I climbed from the car. I ran quickly to the entrance. Tim's family stood, waiting for me near the ticket counter. I had to wait to enter the course, because Dad had the tickets. While Tim's family and I waited for Dad, we cracked jokes together. After Dad caught up, our parents let us play our own miniature golf game.

On my first shot, I had trouble getting the ball in the hole. It took four swings to get it there.

Tim, with his almost perfect swing, got his ball in the hole with two strokes. By the second hole, I knew I was in trouble. Tim made a hole in one, and there was no way I could catch up.

By the time we reached the third hole, I asked Tim for tips to improve. I wanted to become a better player, so I listened to him carefully.

"Try to keep your arm straight. Your ball will land in the hole with fewer strokes," Tim said.

"Thank you for the tip," I replied.

Before I pushed the club toward the ball again, I straightened my arm. On the next round, Tim hit his ball three times before it landed in the hole. As the game continued, it took fewer swings for me to get the ball in each hole. By the last round, Tim still had fewer strokes. But, I knew I was improving.

While Tim and I waited for our parents, Tim gave me other golf tips. I wanted to play another round, but after checking with Dad, there wasn't enough time. The park closed at ten

o'clock. It was already a quarter before ten. As Tim and I split

up, I thanked him for his tips. We agreed to meet by the hotel

steps the next day. I didn't look forward to leaving the beach or

Tim behind. I did look forward to seeing Allie, Jake, and Ben,

though.

Chapter

27

The phone rang early the next morning. Tim talked so fast that I had trouble understanding him. "My dad plans to go fishing today. We're leaving in two hours. Would your family like to go?"

"Yes. That sounds like fun. Hold on. I'll ask my parents."

"I'll wait, but hurry," Tim said.

I explained the fishing trip to my parents. When they said that we could go, I screamed with excitement.

"Hurrah! I'll be ready shortly."

I dashed back to the phone with the good news. My

parents and I threw on our clothes to go out the door. We grabbed a sausage biscuit from a drive-through restaurant for breakfast. Dad filled up our food chest with ice, drinks, and sandwiches for lunch.

On our arrival at the marina, my family took a tour of Tim's family's boat. As the boat pulled away from the moorings, Tim and I watched it cut through the water. We played games until the boat stopped at a fishing area. Then, Tim and his father taught me how to use a fishing rod. While Tim and I fished, we enjoyed talking and laughing together. Even though I hadn't cleared it with Mom, I invited Tim to our house. Mom liked to have company. I knew she'd agree for him to come before the end of the year. I hoped he'd be able to come for the Christmas holidays.

While I waited for a fish to bite my line, I saw Tim's pole bend, like he had caught something. I ran over to help him, as he struggled with his pole.

"Thanks," he said.

Before we pulled the fish in, Tim's rod bent more; I thought it would break, but it didn't. As the fish swung from the rod, we managed to bring it in together. Tim grasped the hook from the fish's mouth, and I helped hold the fish. We put the fish in a barrel filled with ice. Tim and I didn't have a chance to catch other fish before a storm was brewing. When I took my rod to the storage area, I almost lost my balance. The waves hit the boat, making it rock back and forth.

After Tim's father noticed the storm getting worse, he ordered everyone but Dad to the berth area. From his facial expression and voice tone, I knew to move quickly.

The waves splashed and spewed on Tim and me. As the storm became worse, everyone but the two fathers was inside the berth area. I tried not to be afraid, but my legs kept shaking. I didn't like having my dad and Tim's dad out in the storm. The rocking back and forth of the boat made it hard to keep my balance, so I knew it was hard for our fathers to keep their balance, too. The waves kept increasing in size and intensity. The slippery deck had to be hard to walk on.

Once we arrived at the dock, Dad helped Tim's father secure the boat. While they wrestled with the anchor and ropes, the rest of us rushed inside a restaurant for shelter. Tim and I stood inside, watching our fathers remove the families' personal items. The waves continued to rise. The ocean became a terrifying place. At that moment, it was no fun to watch our dads work in the storm. When Dad came inside the restaurant, I questioned him about the storm.

"Do you think we are safe inside the restaurant?"

"It's fairly safe," Dad said.

"Could the waves break the glass here?" I asked.

"It could happen. But, it's unlikely. The storm is weakening, so we're through the worst part. Don't worry," Tim's father said.

"The storm frightened me," I said.

"We get a lot of storms in this area. Weather reports help us stay safe," Tim's father said.

During dinner, we didn't mention the storm. Tim and I kidded each other about games we'd played before. As we parted for the evening, we made plans for Tim to visit my house in the winter. Each family member told the other family members "good-bye" for the summer.

Even though it was late when we returned to the hotel, I

called Jake's number. I wanted to check on Allie, but no one answered at Jake's. That was unusual, because he usually watched television at night. I decided to wait a few minutes, and then call Jake again. My plans didn't work out; I fell asleep.

The next morning, I helped my parents pack the car. By the time we ate and left, it was already ten o'clock. As we drove down the road, I punched in Jake's phone number. Jake still didn't answer his phone.

During the early part of our trip, Dad stopped only for potty breaks. When we stopped for lunch, I leaped from the car. I stepped inside the restaurant, heading to the souvenirs. I didn't get far before Mom stopped me. She reminded me that we were there to eat. I had to go to the lunch area. All during the meal, I stared at the books and toys on display, hoping to browse at the souvenirs. Dad's serious face, all during lunch, indicated he was in no mood to shop.

"We need to get on the road, Matt," Dad said, when I lingered behind.

"Oh, won't you stay a little longer?" I begged.

"You have ten minutes. If you can't find something by

then, you won't get anything. So, look around quickly."

When we'd entered the restaurant, I'd noticed the plastic alligators in the souvenir area. I rushed to look at them. I wanted a real baby alligator, but there were none for sale; I purchased a plastic one.

After my family and I left the shop, I drew a body of water to put my plastic alligator in. For a few minutes, I played with the alligator. Playing with it on a piece of paper wasn't like putting it in water. When Dad questioned me about reaching Jake, I punched in his number again. I set the alligator and picture away. By the time I'd reached Jake, he had disturbing news.

"Allie got loose at the library. When a library patron opened the door, Allie bolted out. She disappeared. We're still looking for her," Jake said.

I sat in a daze. For a few seconds, I said nothing.

"Are you there, Matt?" Jake asked.

"Yes, I'm here. I'll help find Allie when we get home. We can't disappoint people, looking for Allie at our library and school visits. That dog means the world to me. We must find it."

"I know. I'm sorry Allie got loose," Jake said.

"I can't look for the dog right now. We're fifty miles away," I said.

"I'll keep looking as long as it's light outside. I don't think Allie wandered far," Jake said.

When Jake and I finished talking, Mom wanted to know what was going on with Allie. I told her about Allie's escape. Mom tried to comfort me, but I wanted to be left alone.

"Allie always comes home. I think the dog will find its way back. Don't worry. Jake will help look for the dog," Mom said.

"Thanks, Mom," I said, brushing the tears away.

During the remainder of the trip home, I tried to read. My mind wasn't on the book, though. It was on Allie. As the sky blackened, I fell asleep.

Right before our arrival at home, Mom woke me up. Even though I was half asleep, Dad needed help with the family suitcases. I rubbed the matter from my sleepy eyes; I wanted to see well, without a film over my eyes. Once the car halted, I stepped outside to help Dad. Mom sent me to bed after the car was unloaded. When I woke up the next morning, everything seemed to be back to normal, except that Allie didn't greet me.

Chapter

28

When I reached for the phone to call Jake, Mom stopped me. I wondered why she didn't want me to call him then. I needed to know if he'd found Allie.

"I know you need to talk to Jake, but eat breakfast first. Jake probably isn't awake yet. By the time you eat and dress, he'll probably be up," Mom said.

I didn't realize it was only eight o'clock. I would have to wait to call him. When I punched in Jake's number later, no one answered his phone. I waited a few minutes before trying his number again. A voice came on the line that I didn't recognize.

The number I punched in wasn't Jake's, so I apologized. I tried Jake's number again. I breathed a sign of relief after he answered.

"Hi," Jake said.

"Jake, have you found Allie?" I asked.

"No. The dog hasn't shown up yet," Jake answered. "I looked for it, but I needed a break. I came home to get a snack before looking again."

"Our family arrived late last night. If I head out now, we could probably meet at the corner of Oak and Pine Streets. We'll have a better chance of finding the dog, if we look together," I suggested.

"That sounds like a good plan. I'll eat my snack and leave, so I'll be at the corner before long. Good-bye," Jake said.

I ran to the door after I had Mom's permission to leave. Before opening the door, Mom gave me some instructions. I didn't listen as closely as I needed to, because I had to find Allie. In my running shoes, I zoomed down the sidewalk, slamming the screen door behind me.

"Don't slam the door," Mom called out.

I didn't take time to say anything. My apologies to Mom would have to wait until the evening.

It took me eight minutes to arrive at Oak Street. I arrived before Jake, but soon he darted toward me. We discussed where to look; afterwards, we began our search.

At the end of an hour, Jake and I had searched ten blocks. In twenty-five minutes, I had to be home. I asked Jake to help me look in two last places: the school and the library.

"We can look in both places," Jake said. "I checked around the school yesterday. We'll look there again."

"While I'm at home for lunch, I'll try to think of other places to search. Will you help me look after lunch?"

"I think I'll be able to," Jake said.

"I'll call you after lunch. We'll discuss where to look then."

As Jake and I walked around the school together, the grounds looked different than they'd looked before summer vacation. Flowers of every color were in full bloom now; earlier in the spring, buds were just sprouting. Volunteers had planted the flowers. Even though Jake and I admired them, we didn't spend too much time there; we had to find Allie.

While we searched for the dog, I shared my vacation events with Jake. Even though we searched the playground and wooded areas, we didn't find Allie. We heard an unusual sound a couple of times, but we didn't find the source of the noise. When we retraced our steps, I saw a squirrel rush toward a tree, and then a dog appeared. I didn't know whether the dog was Allie or not. It looked like Allie, but I wasn't sure.

Jake and I followed the dog for twenty feet. At first, we had trouble keeping up with the retriever. Once the squirrel disappeared, the dog came toward us. I knew it had to be Allie, because of the way the dog flew into my arms, and it wagged its tail. As Jake and I petted the dog, we discovered a cut on its body. I dug my cell phone from my pocket, and I punched in Mom's number for help. Since Mom understood our problem, she agreed to meet us at the school. When Mom arrived, she helped us put Allie in the car.

"The vet is waiting for us at his office," Mom said. "I phoned him before I left. He will see Allie in a few minutes. I called your mother, Jake. She gave permission for you to go to the vet's office with us."

"Do you think Allie's cut is serious, Mom?" I asked.

"Allie's wound doesn't seem too deep. The vet will check it out."

"Matt wanted to look around the school for Allie," Jake said. "I didn't want to look there, because my father and I had searched there before. The dog wasn't there yesterday."

"Dogs can move along fast," Mom said. "I'm glad you boys found Allie."

As soon as Dr. Thompson examined the retriever, he said, "Allie's been through a few mud holes. The dog's wound isn't serious. I'll clean and disinfect it. Apply this medicine for seven days. Allie should get better soon. Take good care of your dog, Matt."

"Thank you for helping Allie," Mom told Dr. Thompson. "I'm sure the boys feel relieved, since Allie has some reading appearances to make."

"I'm glad the dog's wound isn't serious. The kids like Allie," I said.

"What plans have you boys been making?" asked

Dr. Thompson.

Jake shared our plans, and I grabbed Allie's leash. Both of us scratched and petted Allie, as the dog lifted one paw for us to stroke it.

"I know you will be busy with your pet, Matt. Have fun. This retriever is a great dog," Dr. Thompson said.

"Now, we'll be able to take Allie to the reading events, won't we Mom?"

"I think so. If there are no date conflicts, we should be able to make all the events. Right now, let's take care of Allie, so the dog will heal. We'll get Allie groomed later," Mom said.

"Is it all right to brush Allie?" I asked.

"Yes. Be sure to avoid brushing the wounded area until it heals," Mom said.

On the way home, we made Allie as comfortable as possible. We petted Allie all the way. The way the dog held its huge brown eyes, looking back and forth between us, indicated it was content. Allie's curled mouth looked like it was smiling at us.

Once the car stopped in our driveway, Jake and I hurried

out. We took Allie to the backyard. Inside the fence, we saw the dog dart to retrieve its toy squirrel. I saw Allie pick it up, and then the dog dropped it. I threw the toy squirrel, and Allie retrieved it in an instant. On Jake's throw, Allie clamped down on the toy squirrel with its teeth.

"Drop it, Allie!" I commanded.

Allie obeyed immediately. Once Jake and I threw the toy squirrel several more times, the dog dashed to return it. As soon as Jake reached for it another time, Allie ran away with the toy. I gave the dog a command to stop, and Allie did. When we got closer to the dog, though, it took off running.

"That's one funny dog," Jake stated. "Does Allie just do that with me? Or does the dog do it with everyone?"

"Allie usually chases the toy a couple of times. My dog brings it back to me most of the time, but sometimes Allie does the same thing with me," I said.

"I know one way to get Allie to respond," Mom said.

"What's that?" Jake questioned.

"Allie knows what the word treat means. If you mention a treat, the dog will sit right down."

"I don't have any right now. I'll get two to put inside my pocket," I told Jake.

"Allie needs her regular food and water for the evening. I don't think your dog needs treats until later," Mom told me.

"Jake, would you like to help feed Allie?" I asked.

"I'll help. When we finish, I have to go home. I don't want my mom to be upset."

"You may call your mom to see if you can play longer. Tell her I can drive you home later," Mom suggested.

"I can walk. It's not far."

"Well, I'll drive you. It will be dark soon. Oh! We haven't paid you for taking care of Allie during our vacation," Mom said.

"I don't feel right to take anything, since Allie went missing for a while."

"Allie likes to dig and play. It's easy for a dog to dig its way out, if there is a large enough space. Allie wants to be with the kids who are reading and playing," Mom said.

Jake nodded. "Allie certainly does."

"Allie wandered into our reading group several times," I chimed in.

"You boys can play for twenty minutes," Mom said. "I'll let you know when it's time to take Jake home."

Jake and I practiced baseball in the front yard. We laughed and joked about how the dog liked to chase balls and toys.

"It's time to put all your equipment away," Mom announced after a while. "When you start walking toward the car, I'll join you. Jake's mother wants him to come home now. She will be serving dinner soon."

Once the baseball equipment was stored in the right place, we walked toward the car.

"Mom, would you let Jake tell Allie good-bye?" I asked.

"If you boys can do it quickly, you may go pet the dog," Mom said.

We walked to the backyard to pet Allie. I was glad Allie was home again, but I was sorry to see Jake have to leave.

When we arrived at Jake's house, I followed him to his front door. Before I left, we decided on a time to meet the next day. We wanted to practice for Allie's school and library visits.

➤

Chapter

29

Between archery and baseball, I was busy. I practiced every day

to get ready for the archery competition and the baseball games.

Dog training and household chores took much of my time, too.

Finally, the archery competition day arrived.

When I started to shoot my arrows, perspiration dribbled

down the back of my shirt. My forehead dripped beads of sweat.

To cool down, I gulped water from my insulated bottle. The

temperatures were higher than normal for this time of year.

Drinking the water made me feel better, but I still felt clammy

and nervous.

As I pulled the bowstring back, it felt heavy. I took extra time to aim at the target. Once I released the last arrows of the first end, they landed right inside the bull's-eye, making me feel more confident. The cheering crowd pumped me up. I sat down, and I watched the other competitors shoot. Only two competitors had scores as high as mine after the first end. One of the highest scorers, of course, was Jake. Another boy named Michael had a higher score than mine. I'd never seen him play before today. Three other boys in the competition had scores lower than mine. Ben was fourth in the competition.

I found it tough to compete against my friends in the competition. Jake and Ben showed how good they were during our practices. I knew their strengths and weaknesses. Throughout each end, I looked carefully at the target, keeping my arm steady and straight. On the third end, I misjudged the target point for one of my arrows. It almost went off the board. *Why hadn't I watched and moved more carefully? My clumsy attempt could cost me the tournament.*

The competition continued. I watched closely as Michael's arrow shot through the air, landing on the bull's-eye.

At that moment, I realized what I had to do to stay in the competition. I had to hit the bull's-eye as much as possible, if I wanted to finish in the top three. During the rest of the competition, I concentrated on the things Coach Brown had taught me. I stepped forward for the last end with a positive attitude. To make the points I needed, I tuned out everything around me.

When my friends screamed, I became excited. I had made another bull's-eye. The tension I'd felt earlier had disappeared. The practices and positive attitude kept me in the competition. Whether I won or not, I knew I'd keep doing my best.

During the last end, Jake and I were tied for first place. To break the tie, I needed terrific shots. As I waited to finish my turn, the sun blinded me. I reached for my sunglasses from my T-shirt pocket. With my glasses on, I took aim and released one arrow. This time, fear gripped me. I didn't look ahead to see where the arrow had landed. But, immediately, the crowd roared. My arrow had hit the bull's-eye. The sunglasses had helped me. I wanted to make another bull's-eye. For the next shot, I carefully took aim, releasing the arrow. I didn't look at the board right away, because I was afraid. When the crowd roared again, I looked at the target. I grinned after releasing two more great shots. Then, two of my arrows didn't land where I wanted them to land.

I didn't dwell on my mistakes very long; I wanted to see Jake's shots. Even though I liked to see my friends do well, I wanted to win the competition. The scores Jake received created a tie between us. The judges decided we would have another end to break the tie.

I didn't want to have to shoot again. The sun's glare and the heat made it hard to concentrate. I reached for an arrow, but it slipped from my hand. I didn't want the judges to disqualify me. The spectators didn't cheer for me; they booed me. I tuned the negative reactions out. When I shot again, I was surprised to see the arrow hit the bull's-eye. The other four arrows landed close, but they didn't hit the bull's-eye.

When Jake shot his first arrow, he didn't drop his like I'd done. He didn't hit the bull's-eye, though. His second arrow barely missed it. When he shot three more arrows, they flew through the air, hitting the bull's-eye. The crowd cheered loudly.

His last arrow barely missed the bull's-eye.

I hoped I wouldn't receive a penalty for dropping my arrow. The possibility existed, but I was happy. I thought that I might have one of the winning places in the competition.

As it turned out, Michael won third place; I won second. Jake was the winner.

I had yearned to win the archery contest, but I knew the competition was fierce. In other contests, I'd placed first. I realized I couldn't win every time. I had wanted to win, but this time I hadn't won. I did have the best dog in the world, though. That meant more than winning the archery competition. I could always compete next year.

I shook Jake's hand and congratulated him. I was a little disappointed when I dropped my arrow, but winning second place wasn't so bad.

Jake turned to me. "Are we practicing tomorrow for the yearly competition?" he asked.

"Let's take a break for a week. We can practice after that," I said.

"Suit yourself, but tomorrow I'll be practicing. The

tournament almost ended in a tie. I can't let that happen again," Jake said.

"Practice helps, but it doesn't keep anyone from making a mistake. I know I did my best," I said.

"You might be right. Will I see you later today for baseball practice?" Jake asked.

"I'll be there," I said.

➤

Chapter

30

The summer days flew by. Jake and I continued our practice sessions in archery. Without school being in session, we set up target areas at my house and Jake's. We wanted to be ready for the next yearly competition.

For the remaining summer days, Jake and I not only practiced archery, but we played baseball, walked Allie, and visited the library. We swam several times a week.

When it was time for Allie's next appearance at the library, our parents joined us. Jake and I sat up front with Allie. We wanted to see everything Allie did. Even though we had to wait for Allie to come onstage, I looked forward to seeing my dog. Allie was the summer reading mascot.

Allie sat beside me during the show. I checked on my dog several times to be sure Allie behaved. Every time I looked at Allie, I thought my dog was watching the show. I became so absorbed in the puppet show that I didn't check on Allie for a while. When I turned to check on my dog, Allie had slipped away. I leaned toward Jake to ask a question.

"Jake, did you see Allie leave?" I whispered.

"No. I'll help you look for the dog. Let's hurry before Allie has to go on the stage."

Jake and I stood to search for Allie. Before we left the building, I spotted Allie on the stage, grabbing a dog puppet in its mouth. When Jake and I ran toward Allie to release the puppet, my dog leaped away.

I thought retrieving the puppet wouldn't be so hard, with two of us chasing Allie. It turned into a fiasco. Each time we got close to my dog, it tightened its grip on the puppet. Then, Allie would run just from our reach. I didn't know what to do, but try a simple command.

"Drop," I said.

Once Allie let the puppet go, I grabbed it. I held it up high, away from Allie.

"Good dog," Jake said, as he scratched under Allie's neck.

I walked toward the actor to return the puppet. Before I took two steps, I felt something hit my back foot. The thump startled me, so I turned around. As Allie leaped for the puppet, I raised my arm higher again, keeping it from my dog's clutches. I placed the puppet in the actor's hand, apologizing. While I walked off the stage, the director, Mr. Sims, motioned for me to stop and see him. I walked over quickly, because I knew he was busy.

"I'd like for your dog to be in the next scene if you don't mind," Mr. Sims said.

I wanted Allie to do it, but I didn't know if my dog would behave or not. Allie liked to get frisky. Even though my dog's antics concerned me, I handed Allie over to Mr. Sims. I told him how Allie liked to play games, but he just smiled.

"I've got a dog something like Allie at home. I think your

dog will be the star of the show, no matter what Allie does," Mr. Sims said.

I sat down, but I was uneasy. During the first act, Allie turned out to be a star. I clapped loudly, along with the rest of the audience, when the act ended.

During the intermission, I took Allie outside for a walk. Allie pulled the leash and sniffed the surroundings while Jake and I talked.

"Weren't you proud of Allie?" Jake asked.

"Yes. I was afraid my dog might grab another puppet, though. I didn't want that to happen."

"It would be fun to have Allie in the rest of the play," Jake said.

"My dog might have trouble staying still. That could ruin the show for everyone."

"The clapping showed how much the audience liked Allie," Jake said.

I didn't want to risk having Allie in another act. Before the actors returned, I placed Allie beside me, keeping a watchful eye on my dog.

Right before the show started again, the audience shouted, "Allie, Allie!"

I didn't know what was going on. And then, I realized that everyone wanted Allie back in the show.

I walked my dog back on the stage. During Allie's performance, I had sweat running down my back. I felt relieved once the show ended.

During the curtain calls, Allie received a standing ovation. At the end of the show, Allie was presented a doggy basket, filled with treats and toys.

Later, in the parking lot, Jake and I made plans for the next day. We didn't know what things were in store for us; but with Allie, there were no dull moments.

➤

Chapter

31

When the doorbell sounded, I headed to the door in my pajamas.
I invited Jake in to share breakfast with us. Mom kept plenty of
food around, and I offered Jake eggs, bacon, and toast. He liked
Mom's cooking, so I set him a plate at the table.

"Thanks. I'll eat a bacon strip," Jake said. "I just ate an
hour ago. I came over to discuss Allie's visits to promote
reading."

"Go ahead; tell me your ideas," I said.

Jake and I discussed the program, while we ate. I made a
quick check of Mom's calendar on the kitchen table. I wanted to

be sure nothing else was scheduled on Allie's performance days.

While I brushed my teeth, Jake played with Allie. I wanted to hurry. We had to make plans, but we needed to practice archery and baseball, too.

I threw on my clothes. Jake and I decided to play with Allie for a few minutes. We played fetch with my dog, and then walked Allie around the block. As we opened the gate to put Allie inside, Ben joined us. We talked together for a few minutes, and we agreed to meet later for our practices. Then, Jake and I went inside to plan Allie's next visit.

Once we entered my bedroom, I grabbed my notebook and pen. I wrote down our ideas for the dog's visit. As soon as we finished the school plans, I entered them into the computer. Jake continued writing ideas for other visits.

"Do you think we need a special costume for Allie?" I asked.

"Like a reading dog costume?"

"Yes. Where can we get one?"

"We can make one with a marker, needle, thread, and fabric," Jake said. "Mom showed me a little about sewing. Does your mom keep sewing things around?"

"I think so."

"Making a costume won't take much time," Jake said.

"Let me ask Mom about the materials."

"Wait. Before you go, I need paper and a tape measure, too," Jake said.

I gathered the sewing materials. We finished most of the costume before Jake had to leave.

I added glue and glitter to the costume; afterwards, I set it aside for the glue to dry. While I waited, I read from my library book. As soon as I tried the costume on Allie, my dog sunk its teeth into it. I used a simple command to stop Allie. I smiled when Allie pranced around in the costume. It looked like a store-bought one. A single question remained in my mind: *would the costume last for all the events?* I didn't know, but I knew how to make another one.

I wanted Jake to see the costume, so I rushed out the door. Before I left the yard, Mom stopped me.

"I'm going to show Allie's costume to Jake," I said.

"Why do you have Allie's leash? I thought Jake helped

make the costume," Mom said.

"Jake left before we finished it."

"You don't need Allie to show off the costume."

"But, I wanted Jake to see Allie in it," I replied.

"You didn't ask for permission to leave. Call Jake to cancel your plans," Mom announced.

"Oh, Mom, please let me go. Jake and I have to prepare for Ms. Winthrop's reading celebration."

"Well, you'll have to do it another day. When you disobey, you are grounded for the day. You must ask for permission to do things before leaving."

"Mom, that's not fair!" I shouted.

"Yes, it is. You made the choice."

"Will you let me phone Jake?"

"Call him, but be off the phone in five minutes. I want you to clean your room," Mom said.

I knew I'd made a mistake, but I didn't look forward to telling Jake. He sounded disappointed when I told him what had happened.

"Do you think we can get together tomorrow?" Jake

questioned.

"I'll ask Mom if you can wait."

"Go ahead. I'll wait, but don't take long."

I left my room to search for Mom. When I found her, I asked about visiting with Jake the next day. Her reply surprised me.

"If you follow the rules, you may go. You make the choice," Mom announced.

That was an easy decision for me. I planned to go, so I told Jake to expect me. I told him what Mom had said.

"I'll see you tomorrow. Don't get grounded," Jake said.

"I have to hang up now, so I won't be over my time limit."

"Good-bye," Jake said.

The next day Jake didn't call, so I called him. Before starting to Jake's house, I received Mom's permission.

I whistled to get Allie's attention, but my dog wasn't visible. Something had to be wrong. Allie always greeted me. I opened and closed the gate. As Allie lumbered toward me, I knew I must have awakened my dog. I watched Allie move to be sure my dog wasn't hurt or sick.

I started walking with Allie. At first, my dog almost pulled me down. I tried coaxing Allie on when my dog stopped for too long. Soon, it circled around, marking its territory. I frowned as it made the grassy, curb area its restroom. I had no materials for getting the waste up, so I started home. A scooper was needed. When I tried to get Allie to move, my dog just sat for a minute. I didn't know whether Allie was sick or stubborn. I lifted Allie into my arms. When my arms grew tired from holding my dog, I set it down. This time, I was able to get it to walk ahead. Once I reached home, I called Jake to explain why I wasn't there.

Jake listened to my explanation. He told me that he was willing to come over if his mom didn't mind. I hoped his mother's answer would be a "yes." I knew Jake liked dogs from the way he took care of Allie.

Even though Jake had only two hours to stay, we wanted to try on Allie's costume. I didn't want to put the costume on my dog right away, so we waited. I wasn't sure whether the dog was sick or not. During our waiting period, we worked on our programs. Before going outside, I pulled out Allie's costume to show Jake.

"I like the costume. We'll have a star for the shows," he said.

"I hope so."

Once Jake and I decided to leave the front yard, we left Allie's costume in Mom's rocking chair. For an hour, we played baseball. Before Jake had to leave, we returned to the porch to get the dog's costume.

After we climbed the steps, I reached for Allie's costume from the rocking chair; the chair was empty. Jake and I didn't know where it was.

"I left the costume here, didn't I?"

"Yes. Perhaps your mom put it away," Jake said.

I dashed inside with Jake following. We hunted for the costume in every room. We checked with Mom, but she didn't know where it was, either. Jake and I didn't find the costume anywhere; it seemed to have disappeared.

Jake and I decided to search the yard for the costume. For fifteen minutes, we searched outside. When we started to make the costume over, I spotted it in a cat's mouth. As I reached down to grab the outfit, the cat ran under the porch. Before the cat was out of sight, Jake and I tried to grab it. We missed catching the cat by a foot.

Even though we waited twenty minutes for the cat, it stayed under the porch. Since there wasn't space to crawl under there, Jake and I sat, waiting. When we started to leave, the cat appeared. The cat scurried down the street, moving so swiftly that we were not able to keep up. When the cat finally set the costume down, I bolted ahead. Before the animal took off with the costume again, I grabbed it.

I looked at the costume and checked for holes in it. There were none. That surprised me, since the cat had the costume in its mouth for a long time. I breathed a sigh of relief when I realized that Jake and I didn't have to remake the costume.

"I'm placing the costume in my room," I said. "I'm not taking a chance on losing it again."

Jake looked puzzled. "I'd like to see the costume on Allie, if your dog is healthy."

"Oh, we can check to see if Allie's better."

As soon as Jake and I got close to my dog, Allie swished its tail back and forth. I could tell that Allie felt better by the way the dog acted.

"I see you've found Allie's costume," Mom said.

"A cat had it. I pulled it out of the cat's mouth in the nick of time. I'm going to try it on Allie. I think Allie's feeling better," I said.

"Allie seems fine to me," Mom agreed.

Jake and I struggled to get Allie in the costume. The word on the costume stood out in bold letters: the word was *read*.

"I know Ms. Winthrop will like Allie's costume with the word read on it," I said.

"The word stands out in bold letters. It looks beautiful. I promised my mom I'd get home on time, so I'd better leave. We can practice the program for Ms. Winthrop's class tomorrow," Jake said.

I returned to my room. As fast as the ideas popped in my head, I jotted them down for the next program. By the time I'd finished the list, I had seven more ideas to use.

➤

Chapter

32

The next day, I had a new idea for Allie's school program. I wanted to teach Allie to bark when I said the word read. While I sat at a bedroom table, I thought of a poster concept to use for reading. I gathered my supplies. I printed the poster title: "Reading Opens Doors for You." When I finished the title, I drew a huge door with many possible book choices inside it. I was pleased with the way it turned out. I hadn't been able to think of any ways to get Allie to bark at the right time, though.

I called a dog expert, Seth, to learn training tips for Allie. When I tried some of his tips, things didn't go like I'd planned. I decided to take a break. During the break, I read from my library book.

When Jake showed up, I didn't know whether to mention my new plans or not. My dog didn't always bark at the right time. I shared my idea with Jake anyway. I thought he might be able to help me with the dog.

"I'd like for my dog to bark every time I say the word read, but Allie doesn't always do it. When I want Allie to bark on cue, I can use a treat. Will you wait while I get some treats? You could jot other ideas down for us."

I hurried to the laundry room for Allie's treats. I pushed five small ones inside my pocket. Every time, Jake and I got Allie to bark at the right time, we gave the dog a treat.

When Allie's second training session ended that day, Jake and I walked to my room. Before I had a chance to share my other plans with him, Jake saw the poster board on my desk.

"What's that poster board for?" Jake asked.

"I bought it for our programs," I said.

I showed him the poster I'd started. Then, I explained that we could make other posters.

"That sounds like a good idea. I'll try to think of other poster slogans," Jake said.

"Do you have another title now?"

"We can brainstorm together. I need a smaller sheet of paper to use, so I don't ruin the poster board sheets."

"Here's a large tablet. Will that work?" I asked.

"Yes. Now, we can record ideas and draw sketches."

I took a few sheets from the tablet, and I let Jake use the rest of it. For several minutes, Jake and I wrote down ideas. We shared our thoughts with each other after fifteen minutes.

"Tell me what you think of this title: 'Through Reading You Learn About the World,' " Jake said.

"I like your caption."

"I'll draw a world map to go with the second poster," Jake said.

"I have a third idea. 'Keep Your Brain Working: Read.' We could draw the brain parts inside of a head outline."

"That's the best title yet. You know boys will like it. Of course, some girls might scream, seeing the brain parts," Jake remarked.

"A few will, but most girls will think it is all right."

"Well, we want to get everyone to read. Do you think we should change our idea?"

"I like the idea. We can each draw two posters, but we need to get busy. There's not much time to finish them. We can always make more if there's time."

"I'll get Mom's medical book for the brain parts and the labels."

"Before you go, let me give you a fourth caption: 'Reading Entertains People With Stories About the Past or Future.' Do you like that one?"

"I think it will be a good one, too. We each have two captions for our next program," I said.

"Wouldn't it be fun to go to the library? We'd have more space to spread out on the large tables," Jake said.

"Let me ask Mom about going."

"If your mom agrees for you to go, I'll call mine. I'll begin on one poster while you ask for permission to go."

By the time I'd returned to the room, Jake had one picture drawn. I gave him the phone to call his mother. Once he had permission to go to the library, we gathered all our materials to work.

Jake and I didn't want to waste time, so we hurried to the library. We set our materials on a table. Then, we searched for several pictures to help us with our posters. I made a poster from the brain picture, and Jake worked on another poster. Without stopping, we worked for over an hour. The librarian only had to give us a little help.

Every now and then, I saw the head librarian, Mrs. Lindsey, glance at our project. Within a few minutes, she walked over and complimented us on our work. I took a few minutes to tell her more about our project.

"We're taking my dog to a reading celebration at school. We want kids to learn to like reading," I explained.

"You boys helped our reading program this summer. I know you will help at your school. The posters will add to your presentation," Mrs. Lindsey said.

"Thank you," Jake and I replied.

"I will be glad to assist you if you need me," Mrs. Lindsey said.

"Thanks for offering to help," Jake said.

By the time we finished drawing the pictures, it was time to go home. We hurried along, to avoid getting into trouble.

On the way home, Jake wanted to stop by the store. He didn't think it would take more than five extra minutes. I agreed to stop, since he wanted an ice cream sandwich. Once we found the right store aisle, we chose a package of them. I agreed to help pay for the ice cream sandwiches, since I planned to eat some of them. I decided that I could put the leftover ice cream into Mom's freezer. There was one problem with our plan: it was ninety degrees outside. By the time we got home, I rushed to get the ice cream sandwiches into the freezer. I didn't notice that some of the ice cream had melted. It had landed on Mom's kitchen floor.

When Jake left, I rushed to wash my hands in the bathroom. Once I returned to the kitchen, I found Mom staring at the floor. I realized there was a huge problem when I heard Mom's commanding voice.

"When you drop something on the floor, you need to clean it up," Mom said. "Here's the mop and the cleaning solution."

"What did I do?"

"You dropped something white and sticky on the kitchen floor," Mom answered.

"I'm sorry, Mom."

"What did you get on the floor? Where did you get it?" Mom asked. "I thought you went to the library."

"We stopped at the grocery store on the way home."

I realized I'd said the wrong thing after I'd spoken. I hadn't asked for permission to stop at the store.

"Tomorrow you are grounded," Mom announced.

"Oh, no, Mom. Jake and I need to work on the school project."

"You'll have to work by yourself tomorrow. If you follow the rules, you and Jake can meet the day after tomorrow."

I put my hands on both cheeks and looked down. Without saying a word, I walked to my room. I knew I should have asked before going to the store, but I hadn't planned to go there. When we left, Jake and I had only planned to visit the library. In the evening, I asked for permission to call Jake.

By the time I'd reached Jake, he had plans for the day after tomorrow. We were forced to work alone for two days on the project. I planned to do my best. I trusted that Jake would work hard, too.

➤

Chapter

33

I stepped out to check on Allie early the next day. I opened the side door to find my dog running close to the fence. My dog greeted me with its doting eyes; Allie swished its tail as well. To give my dog some exercise, I tossed Allie the toy squirrel.

"Fetch," I said.

When I threw the toy several more times, Allie returned it. Each time my dog brought the toy squirrel to me, I rewarded Allie. I rushed inside to work on my posters after the fetch game. Before I began the poster work, Mom stopped me.

"Breakfast is ready. Don't begin your project until we

eat."

"Will you let me work on it after breakfast?"

"Finish dressing, clean your room, and empty the trash. You can work on your project then," Mom said.

By half past nine, I had Mom's chore list completed, so I grabbed a pencil. I added to my rough sketch, but it still needed work. When I tried correcting my mistakes, the poster looked worse. I ripped it into pieces, throwing it away. I grabbed another piece of poster board to start over.

My next sketch turned out better. At the top, I printed the caption words. Before finishing the poster, I took a short break to check on Allie.

As soon as I stepped inside the fence, I discovered a giant hole. I knew Allie had just dug it, since the dirt was loose. To keep someone from falling into the hole, I used a shovel to replace the dirt. Allie wasn't far away while I worked.

When I entered the kitchen, I hoped to avoid Mom's questions. She stared at me as I came in. I didn't want her to know about the hole. I started to my room, but Mom began her questions.

"Where did the dirt come from?" Mom asked.

I hadn't noticed the dirt I'd tracked in. While I explained what had happened, I reached for the broom and dustpan. Frantically, I swept up the dirt. Each time I thought I'd finished, Mom found more dirt. I swept nonstop for ten minutes. Once only a little dirt remained, Mom left the room. I swept the dirt up and put the broom away. I was happy, since I would have no more sweeping to do. I tossed my jeans, shirt, and socks into the laundry room. I darted to my room before anyone could see me in my T-shirt and underpants.

As I showered, Mom called me to lunch. I needed to finish my shower, so I yelled from the bathroom to her; after showering, I dried and dressed myself. I said little to anyone during lunch. I wanted to hurry, so I could return to my room. The posters for Allie's visit needed completing.

With markers, I added color to the pictures and letters. I smeared one letter by mistake, and I stamped my foot in anger. As I stared at the smudge, I decided to ask for mom's correction pen. I brushed the white ink over the smear, and then I waited for it to dry. I wanted the poster to be neat. The last school year, Ms.

Winthrop had stressed doing neat work. When I completed the poster, I called Jake.

"Have you finished your posters for the reading event?" I asked.

"No. I'll finish them soon," Jake said.

"Haven't you worked on either one, since we worked together?"

"What's the big hurry? I can finish them tonight," Jake remarked.

"It took me all afternoon to finish."

"What took you so long?"

"I had to redo one poster. The first sketch didn't look right. Then, I smeared a letter on the second poster, so I covered it up with Mom's correction ink."

"I won't be able to come over tomorrow. My mom's taking me to a special place," said Jake.

"Where?" I asked.

"It's a surprise. Mom hasn't told me yet," said Jake.

"When will you find out?"

"Mom doesn't tell me ahead; she doesn't want to spoil

the surprise."

"Do you need for me to finish the next poster?" I offered. "We need to finish them."

"Did we ever decide what caption to use on it?" Jake asked.

"I think we decided on the caption: 'Reading Entertains People With Stories About the Past or Future.' "

"I'll finish both of my posters. We can meet at my house at ten o'clock the next day," Jake said.

"I don't know if I should leave Allie. When I'm gone, my dog likes to dig."

"Try this idea: put a small wire fence inside the larger fence where Allie's digging. That might keep the dog out," Jake said.

"I might try your idea."

"So, the day after tomorrow, are you coming to my house?" Jake asked.

"If Mom says, 'You may go,' I'll be there."

"I might be able to come to your house if you can't come to mine," Jake said.

"I will call you if I can't come. I'd better hang up, so we'll have time to finish the posters."

At the end of the conversation with Jake, I found additional program information online. For an hour, I worked without stopping on the program. I took a snack break at the end of an hour.

By late afternoon, I had my posters and information ready. To be sure my posters stayed spotless, I cleared my desk to set them on. Then, I was ready to leave for baseball practice.

With my baseball and glove in hand, I searched for Mom. I needed her permission to go to Ben's house. Once Mom agreed for me to leave, I left.

I hurried to Ben's, since several classmates planned to come over. More playing positions would be filled, so I looked forward to the game. I worked hard on my team to win. Near the end of the game, Ben's team led by two runs. Nervously, I stepped up to the home plate. I watched the pitcher throw the ball. When my bat struck the ball, I managed to hit a home run. The player after me hit one as well. Our team was tied with the other team. I didn't want to have to leave the game, but it was time to go. Mom had stressed getting back on time. Before leaving the field, I called time out.

"I'm sorry, fellows. I have to go. Mom told me to be home in eight minutes. I'll have to leave now to make it," I said.

"You can't leave the game now!" Ben shouted. "You're just afraid we might beat your team."

"That's not true. I have to leave now; I don't want to be grounded. You can finish without me."

"Your mom won't care if you are a few minutes late," Ben said.

"Yes, she will. I'm leaving. I can play later in the week. Good-bye."

"Why can't you play two days from now?" Ben asked.

"Jake and I have to practice for Ms. Winthrop's reading event. I'll see you later."

"But we need to finish the game!" Ben shouted.

Even though I wanted to complete the game, I knew I had to go. As I hurried home, a new program idea popped in my head. *A book giveaway might work. We could have two small prizes; each of us could furnish one prize.*

On my arrival at home, I opened the front door to familiar cooking smells. I could tell Mom had cooked my favorite meal: spaghetti.

Without Mom saying a word, I washed my hands and set the table. During dinner, I ate a large portion of spaghetti, and I told about my day.

After dinner, Mom said, "Playing ball made you hungry. Look at your empty plate."

"You made my favorite meal. I liked the ice cream dessert, too. It cooled me down."

"We have more ice cream sandwiches in the freezer. You may have one tomorrow," Mom said. "Don't eat one too close to a meal, though."

"Thanks, Mom. I'll have one tomorrow."

I returned to my room after dinner. I took a bath, so I'd be ready for my favorite show on television. While I put on my pajamas, I decided that a game might work for the giveaway. Kids enjoyed playing games, so if one wasn't expensive I planned to buy it. Of course, kids also liked receiving books as presents. Even though I checked out books from the library, I liked owning my own books. Kids might like to have their own books, too.

I planned to discuss the prizes with Jake later. Jake liked sharing ideas about the reading events. He also had a soft spot for Allie, so I knew he looked forward to the reading celebration.

Right now, I was heading to the family room. My favorite television show was beginning.

➤

Chapter

34

I mentioned ideas for surprises to Jake during our next meeting time. We needed time to get them, because the event was in two days. My donated prize had to be less than my allowance. I mentioned some possible prizes, and Jake added some to my list. When I checked the online prices, they were higher than what Jake and I wanted to pay. Jake and I decided to wait to purchase anything. For the time being, we practiced our program. As we practiced, an idea came to me for the surprise.

"Maybe our mothers will fix a snack for the class," I suggested. "We could give out two prizes. The two students who answer the most questions about books could get the prizes."

"That's a great idea. Advertising the prizes and refreshments will get everyone excited. My mom makes good lemonade, so perhaps she'll make some for us. Could you bring some chips?" Jake asked.

"I'll ask Mom about the refreshments now. Will you jot down any other ideas?"

"It's easier to type ideas on a computer. My writing isn't that neat," Jake said.

"Come with me, Jake. I'll let you use the computer in the family room."

I looked for Mom while Jake worked on the computer. Before long, I found Mom writing notes to friends and family members. When I entered her room, she gave me her full attention.

"Mom, would you help with refreshments for the school reading event?" I asked.

"What do you need?"

"Cookies, chips, and party mix. Jake is hoping his mother will make lemonade. He hasn't asked her yet."

"I can call her if you'd like," Mom said.

"Could you do it now?"

"Let me finish this card, and then I'll call her."

I started to explain what Mom and I had discussed to Jake, but Mom interrupted us.

"You don't have to worry about the refreshments. I'm calling Jake's mother to discuss them. If she can't help, I'll find someone to help us. I'll leave you boys to work, so you can finish your plans."

"Thanks, Mom," I said.

****

The two days before the program flew by. Jake and I hurried to finish everything. We even washed Allie. With our practice and our props, we felt ready.

On the night before the reading program, Jake slept at my house. We didn't stay up late, like we normally did; we wanted to be ready for the program.

The next morning, Jake and I dressed and ate. When we were ready to leave, we walked outside. Once Mom unlocked the car trunk, Jake and I set our posters inside it. We placed my dog inside the back seat of the car after we put Allie on a leash. When we were settled, Mom drove to Jake's house. We drove there to get Jake's mother, Mrs. Graham, to ride with us to school.

At school, our mothers signed us in at the office. We were surprised to have Mr. Henry walk us down to Ms. Winthrop's room.

Our group stood outside Ms. Winthrop's door, as she welcomed us. She had chairs in the hallway for us to sit in. Ms. Winthrop encouraged us to relax.

"I'll talk to the children before you give your program. I want them to enjoy your visit, but to follow certain rules," Ms. Winthrop said.

"We have the refreshments. When do you want us to set them out?" Mom asked.

"Give me five minutes. You can work on them after that. Until it is time for the program, please keep the dog out. Do you boys need someone to help you with Allie?" Ms. Winthrop asked.

"We can handle my dog," I said.

"I have the room decorated for the event. We may have some visitors. You boys don't mind, do you?" Ms. Winthrop asked.

"No," Jake and I agreed.

"I know you will do well," Ms. Winthrop said. "I saw one of your library presentations, so I'm looking forward to this program."

"I hope all students accept the reading challenge," Mrs. Graham said.

"The reading challenge information is in packets," Ms. Winthrop said. "I think we'll get a good response."

Right before Jake, Allie, and I entered the room, our principal brought visitors from the county education office into Ms. Winthrop's room. Jake and I were ready to begin after everyone was seated. Mom held Allie in the hallway while Mrs. Graham finished setting up the refreshments.

As I introduced the program, my legs shook. They stopped shaking after a few minutes, as I explained the reading challenge. Once Jake started speaking, he was able to keep the kids' attention with his funny jokes. Then, he shared his ideas about reading and his posters with the group. When his program part ended, I presented the posters I'd made for the event. Near the end of the program, I brought my dog into the room with its costume on. When I pointed out the word read on Allie's costume, everyone looked closely. The children started giggling, pointing to my dog's costume. I waited a minute before continuing, because I couldn't compete with the noise. When the children's voices quieted down, I started again.

"I am glad you liked Allie's entrance. I think you'll like what my dog can do," I said.

I held my breath a minute. I wasn't sure whether the dog would do what we'd practiced. Of course, Allie responded like I wanted. My dog barked when I said the word read. I repeated the trick several times. Each time I repeated it, more students signed up for the reading challenge. At the end of four barks, the whole class had signed up.

While Ms. Winthrop thanked us for the program, Jake and I took our seats. Then, Ms. Winthrop told the children to look at the sign on the dog, as she let us march around the room with the dog.

Soon, Ms. Winthrop announced, "Refreshments are ready for everyone."

While some children stood in the refreshment line, I stood in another line with Allie. Even though there was a long refreshment line, the line to see Allie was even longer. The teacher solved our problem by letting small groups pet Allie. She let each group have five minutes to stroke the dog.

As the children petted Allie, I became thirsty. I wanted some refreshments. Jake had finished his refreshments, so I asked him to take over for me. Once I had my refreshments, I moved closer to Allie and Jake. That was a mistake. Before I knew what had happened, Allie had jerked away from Jake. I couldn't catch Allie and hold my plate. Allie bumped into me. My cookie fell off my plate. I couldn't catch it. Right before the cookie hit the floor, Allie leaped, gobbling it up.

"Oh, no, Allie!"

The celebration readers laughed, and the flash on Mom's camera went off. I hoped Mom's picture showed Allie catching the cookie. The cameramen from one of the television stations had taken pictures of the event, too.

The program didn't end like I'd planned it, but everyone clapped for a star pet: Allie. Before we left, the class clapped for our mothers and us.

That evening, Jake and I turned on the television. We found a video of our reading celebration playing on one station. The television producers showed a small section of our program for the viewers. At the end of the video, I smiled when I realized the cameramen had captured great shots of Allie. The pictures of the dog's costume were priceless. The cameramen had also captured Allie leaping for the cookie.

After I saw Mom's printed pictures, I grinned. One picture showed my dog doing what it does best; Allie was catching a treat. I was happy with Allie's performance, and the dog's performance gave the class a terrific reason for reading. They looked forward to Allie's next visit. The children would list the books they'd read before Allie's next visit. During that visit, all the reading list challenges would be turned in. In order to have Allie visit again, children had to have met their reading goals. And I felt like all the kids would meet their goals to see Allie in motion.

Other Books by Patricia Cruzan

Children's Books
Max Does It Again
Molly's Mischievous Dog
Tall Tales of the United States

Poetry Books
My Reflections
Sketches of Life

Available from Amazon.com and other book stores.

Author's Website
www.patriciacruzan.com

Patricia Cruzan has written four children's books and two poetry chapbooks. She has written poems for various anthologies, such as for *The Meaning of Christmas, Poetry of the Golden Generation,* volume IV, and the *World Poetry Movement.*

As a former teacher, Patricia wrote newsletters. Patricia's poems, articles, or stories have appeared in *Focus, Grit* magazine, *Fayette Woman, Fayette Daily News, Today in Peachtree City, and East Coweta Journal.* Some of her photographs have also been published in various publications.

Patricia has won two first places in poetry contests: she won one for Georgia Writers Association in 2008 and one for the World Poetry Movement in 2012. She has also won a second place in overall writing for 2009 from the Georgia Writers Association.

As a child, Patricia loved to play outdoors on swings and bicycles. Her dolls, paper dolls, and dogs consumed a large portion of her playtime as well. She enjoyed making a home for her dolls, outside, in makeshift houses. Her backyard home porch served as the perfect spot for play.

Many of Patricia's childhood hours, when not involved in play activities, were those spent in church. For much of her life, she sang in choirs or choral guilds. She enjoyed singing concerts and solos for many years.

Patricia has lived in various locations throughout the United States, and she has visited England, France, Australia, and Mexico. She was born in Florida, but Georgia has been her home for over fifty years of her life.

24851358R10134

Made in the USA
Charleston, SC
08 December 2013